STORIES
OF THE
SUN

DAWN NELSON

First published 2024

The History Press
97 St George's Place, Cheltenham,
Gloucestershire, GL50 3QB
www.thehistorypress.co.uk

British Library Cataloguing in Publication Data.
A catalogue record for this book is available from the British Library.

ISBN 978 1 80399 095 8

Typesetting and origination by The History Press
Printed and bound in Great Britain by TJ Books Limited, Padstow, Cornwall.

Trees for LYfe

NOT TILL WE ARE LOST, IN
OTHER WORDS, NOT TILL WE
HAVE LOST THE WORLD, DO
WE BEGIN TO FIND OURSELVES,
AND REALIZE WHERE WE ARE
AND THE INFINITE EXTENT OF
OUR RELATIONS.

WALDEN BY HENRY
DAVID THOREAU (1854)

CONTENTS

Foreword by Tiffany Francis-Baker   7

Introduction   9
January – *Tilting at the Sun*   13
February – *The In-Between*   29
March – *Clock Watching*   51
April – *The Hirundines Return*   67
May – *Fire Story*   81
June – *Standstill*   99
July – *Keepers of the Sun*   115
August – *Dog Days*   129
September – *Life-Giver*   145
October – *Adjusting to the Dark*   163
November – *Capturing the Light*   175
December – *Eclipse*   191

Acknowledgements   204
About the Author   205
Bibliography   206
By the Same Author   208

FOREWORD

DAWN AND I HAD BEEN friends for many years by the time we booked tickets to the Stonehenge exhibition at the British Museum. We both live and work in rural Hampshire, but this visit to the heart of London remains one of my favourite days spent in her company. We crossed the river, sipped coffee and chatted our way over to Great Russell Street, then stepped into the world of ancient Britain and her people – into the world of Stonehenge. The whole exhibition was fascinating, but the highlight was being able to see the Nebra Sky Disc with our own eyes. This beautiful bronze disc is thought to be the oldest known map of the night sky, illegally unearthed by detectorists in Germany in the summer of 1999 and dating back almost four millennia. It is decorated with a handful of gold pieces, each believed to represent cosmic bodies like the crescent moon, stars and solstice markers orbiting that bright and blazing goddess of the solar system – our sun.

When I imagine Dawn researching, writing and performing her stories, I think of the disc upon which we both gazed in wonder that day, deep within the walls of the British Museum. The tapestry of Dawn's craft is woven from voices all over the world, and she respects the cultural fabric from which every thread has been spun. But each of the stories she tells is like one of the Nebra stars orbiting the sun. At the heart of it all, these stories are about the very nature of existence; a connection with the earth, with each other, with the past, present and future. Whether it's a Greek myth, a Slavic folktale or an Aztec legend, Dawn possesses the storyteller's wisdom: the knowledge that despite all our differences, whether we are human, non-human or something in between, we are all just trying to understand our place within this mysterious world.

And where better to start than the sun? The beating heart of our world, giving life to everything we see – and, of course, enabling us to see it. It is remarkable to think that a ball of plasma 150 million kilometres away affects every aspect of our lives. Our relationship with the sun is so exquisitely balanced that even a cloud passing between us can make us cold enough for an extra layer. And although modern science has revealed more about solar power than ever before, there is plenty of wisdom in the old stories, too. Stories of birdsong and sarsen stones, midsummer days and solstice nights.

The beauty of this book is in its simplicity. Twelve moments with the sun as it rises and sets, sometimes solitary, sometimes not, but always in the company of the land and its turning seasons. Dawn tracks the changing rhythms of the year and reflects on how we have interpreted the sun's presence, then tunes in more closely still. There is always an unsentimental respect for nature in her writing, because she admires both the light and darkness, the beauty and the sorrow found in the earth. So help yourself to a drink, take a seat by the hearth, and listen to Dawn weave golden-threaded stories of the sun. You will soon see each wildflower, hedgerow and sun-ripened apple in a completely new light.

Tiffany Francis-Baker
Author of *Dark Skies* and *The Bridleway: How Horses Shaped the Landscape*. https://tiffanyfrancisbaker.com

INTRODUCTION

WHEN I WAS A TEENAGER I climbed to the top of the third highest point in England: Helvellyn. This was not the first time I had climbed this particular mountain in the Lake District, but it was the first time I had attempted it at three o'clock in the morning.

Our ascent was in the dark, negotiating the craggy rock face, bleary eyed and heavy with sleep, to bivvy bag on the top and watch the sun come up for the Summer Solstice.

It was an otherworldly experience and I still remember the warm glow of the sun as it started to appear on the horizon, our smiles widening with it and how the light danced on our faces. Sunrise and sunset are magical, liminal spaces and this experience cemented that knowledge within me.

Around ten years later I was working in emergency care and this liminal space was now well known to me. I witnessed many sunrises as my shifts both started and ended. Occasionally the crepuscular creatures of the twilight would cross our paths. The usual deer bounding across the back lanes, badgers thundering through hedgerows, hedgehogs scuttling along the gutters looking for a dropped kerb and, on one occasion, a tawny owl sitting bang in the middle of the road, dazzled by the blue lights.

Another ten years passed and I'm not sure when I became aware of it, but it had suddenly been over twenty years since that sunrise on Helvellyn. I'd had my head down achieving the career I thought was required of me, until I looked up and saw the world differently. I suddenly heard its rhythms in a very real and visceral way, and I saw these patterns very clearly in the stories I read. I devoured the anthologies of Wilhelm and Jacob Grimm, Joseph Jacobs, Giambattista Basile, Madame d'Aulnoy, Charles Perrault and many more. Stories reignited my desire to connect with the liminal spaces in life.

Another ten years, this time full of tales and lore, and now, as a storyteller, I work in a different liminal space; the space between reality and imagination.

When the pandemic hit in 2019, I realised how very privileged I was in having the South Downs on my doorstep, being able to step out into the country for my state-sanctioned exercise. As I walked, the knowledge and rhythms of all those stories that I had been studying, researching, crafting and telling created a bridge between me and the landscape. It spoke to me in a different way and everywhere I looked I saw stories. Stories of green women in the trees, tales of the epic journeys of the swallows and martins, and the lore of the boggarts who lurked beneath the hedgerows.

Through these stories, many voices spanning hundreds of years spoke to me. They spoke their rhythms and cycles over and over. The stories sang to my bones; they were part of me. Taoists refer to this as our ancestral *Qi* (chee). It is the spirit of our relatives and ancestors that we hold within us. We all have it; we're just not necessarily listening. This *Qi* is a connection not just to our ancestors but to the land that we live on and the creatures that we share it with. Stories can help us find our way back to that *Qi*.

I chose to start the Sunrise Project in order to reconnect with the earth during that liminal space in the morning between sleeping and waking. I found a spot that faced east and had a clear view of the sun rising. I returned to this spot once a month for a year and recorded my long sits through nature journalling. I found that whilst I sat there, the stories of the sun also wanted to be heard – the ancestral *Qi* within my bones spoke of the many sunrises and myths, legends and folktales that recorded the power of our largest star. And so it was that I combined my sunrise journals with folklore and stories of the sun to bring you this book.

Before you read any further, I'd like to invite you to stop and listen, wherever you are. If you can, step outside – but if not, where you are is just fine.

Wherever your spot is, sit, stand or lie, however you feel comfortable, and then take a moment to listen. Listen to the hum of any nearby traffic, the susurration of the trees that line the street or the grass of the lawns and verges. Inside the house, you will find similar sounds in the appliances. The hum of the fridge, the thud and splash of the washing in the machine or the ever-so-faint whir of a light bulb. In a coffee shop? You may notice the chink of cups, the hiss of the steamer and friends chatting. Outside in the garden, birdsong perhaps or footsteps on the path, the chit of a spade turning the soil, or a clucking blackbird startled by a cat. Wherever you are, listen for the sounds, find the rhythm of that place.

Now bring it back to you. Listen to your breathing, consciously move the air in and out of your lungs, *feel* its rhythm. Listen to your heart, *hear* its rhythm.

Everything has a rhythm but often we are so focused on the tasks of modern life that they become a part of our subconscious not acknowledged as a necessary part of our being. They continue on within us and around us without us consciously engaging with them, but they are there.

We may even try and push against natural rhythms, such as those of sunrise and sunset, the phases of the moon or the turning of the tides. We may diarise our day, flex the hours that we work with synthetic light, use video calls to connect, but every time we do this, we are ignoring the rhythms our very being knows best. We are fighting against biophilic rhythms.

Within these pages Baba Yaga will show you the source of all light, Sol will ride her chariot many times across the sky, children will travel from the underworld to tell you their tales and flower-faced women will become creatures of the dusk. We will discover dark places, shine light into them and embrace the power of our light source and life force.

The twelve chapters, one for each month, each have a section of nature narrative in the form of a sunrise vigil. These vigils took place over 2021 and 2022. Within these vigils I explore nature, folklore and the stories that connect us with the sun. Each chapter has a story connected to my experiences during that sunrise and an invitation to carry out an activity to help you connect with the stories, the nature and landscape within them and, of course, the sun.

To help you further, as we follow the seasons and the four solar festivals within it, there is a downloadable PDF detailing the wheel of the year, via the website page that accompanies this book. You can also find further resources to help you with the various activities via this page: **www.ddstoryteller.co.uk/stories-of-the-sun**

JANUARY

TILTING AT THE SUN

I SIT IN THE GRASS, damp from yesterday's rain, waiting. Winter's early morning voices have already begun to
sing. Tawny owls call to each other in the trees above my
sit-spot. I have brought with me a flask of coffee and a circular, sweet, orange, tortas biscuit. The sugar sparkles in the
half-light and the orange pieces buried within it are like
the sun I wait for, buried in the morning clouds. The sugary
goodness from the Spanish flat-bread biscuit, once the

favoured snack of stagecoach passengers, gives me much-needed energy. As I hit the alarm this morning to stop it from waking anyone else, the clock read 6 a.m. – a good hour earlier than I usually get up, but still not as early as I know I will have to, in six months' time, in order to continue my planned year of monthly sunrise vigils.

The sky is paint-pot black and the stars are bright. As I walked to the dark spot on the hill I have chosen for this project, everything felt alien. I kept thinking I could hear fellow mammals in the undergrowth when in actual fact it was the rustling of my own clothes.

I am lucky enough to live in a little village nestled in the South Downs National Park, which is an International Dark Skies Reserve. This means that urban skyglow is kept to a minimum through planning and quantifiable guidelines on light levels. In turn this allows the skies above the South Downs to be perfect for star gazing, night hikes and, of course, our nocturnal neighbours.

The village has no street lamps and this, coupled with the new moon, means there is no other light. I was glad of my torch. I could have risen later when the atmospheric light was enough for me to see by, still well before sunrise, but I wanted to experience the shifting in the light, truly immerse myself in the space between night and day.

I am reminded of the stories I have read, listened to and indeed told about the Lincolnshire Carrs. The stretches of boggy marshland that hide all manner of nefarious beings: boggarts, boggles, will o' the wisps, lantern men and disembodied dead hands. The folktale of 'The Buried Moon' tells of a time when the moon is trapped beneath the marshes with nothing to illuminate the night for months on end, until the villagers find a way to join together and free her. I am certainly able to empathise with the characters in these tales as the tree branches reach out of the hedgerows towards me, and the path, slick with mud from last night's rain, sucks at my boots.

Once I find my chosen spot, I turn the torch off and wait. After ten minutes of sitting, the darkness starts to lift and I see a yellow line appear on the horizon. Behind me, in the copse, a tawny owl calls and more soon join it, their k'wik and t'woo contact calls echoing back and forth. Dogs bark in the village below and the light creeps slowly into the sky until there is just one star left above me, trapped in the skeleton crook of a tree's branches.

In the wood, the tawny owls have found each other and their calls crescendo in a happy frenzy of voices until, just as suddenly, there is silence. Tawny owls have a variety of nicknames: brown hoolet, Jenny howlet, hoot owl and, in Sussex, the 'ollering owl. My particular favourite has to be the ferny hoolet, which combines its appearance with its call to create the perfect kenning for a Tawny Owl. The t'wit, t'woo that we classically associate with most owls is actually the contact call of the tawny owl and not just one owl but two. The t'wit or k'wik, as it is more commonly written phonetically, is the female and the t'woo or ho-hoo is the male. The two I had been listening to were a pair: a male and a female. A little early morning love story as the two of them found each other once more before retiring for the day.

As the darkness lifts, the clock strikes seven and the field of the day that I am familiar with comes into view, no longer the dark, unwelcoming expanse that it was as I struggled to find my way to the sit-spot. A finch bobs across my view from one set of trees to the next, its undulating flight unmistakable.

A splash of yellow appears above the trees; I can't be sure if the sun has come up yet or not. I don't think I've been up specifically to watch a sunrise since that morning on

Helvellyn, and whilst I have worked night shifts in the past, I was working. You don't necessarily have time to take in the dawn in all its glory, or even notice the different stages of light and the sun rising.

A cacophony of rooks leave their roost for the day and they wake the collared doves who coo sympathetically.

A robin greets the light loudly and hops down from the tree to drink from a muddy puddle, leaving in a flurry of feathers as soon as it spots me. Shortly after the robin, a blackbird tumbles out of the hedgerow and disappears again, tutting at my presence. It would appear I am sitting a few feet away from the best puddle in the meadow.

The robin in folklore can be quite onerous. This one was certainly cross, if nothing else. It is believed that a robin coming into your house foretells the death of someone in the household. This is true for a robin tapping on your window too. Conversely, the robin also became the subject of a murder mystery in the poem 'Who Killed Cock Robin?' There's not much mystery to the story as the sparrow confesses within the first line; however, the story is well loved and ends in a rather fitting funeral for poor Cock Robin.

Owls are also considered bad omens in folklore, and given my early morning encounters with two dark messenger birds, I'm rather hoping that on this occasion this lore is not correct, and that I make it back down the hill and safely home.

It's almost completely light and it feels like the sun must have come up by now, yet I cannot see it and there are no clouds. I start to doubt myself. Perhaps I am sitting in the wrong place, facing the wrong direction? I check my position on a map. No. I'm facing east. I'm in the right place.

The robin's back and it trills at me as if asking permission to share the puddle. I, of course, acquiesce; it is by no means my puddle and I am pleased he has forgiven me.

It is now almost completely light; there are no more pinks, oranges or yellows in the sky. A Yaffle (green woodpecker) laughs at me from a nearby field. It knows I must be patient and all will be revealed.

At ten past eight, almost ninety minutes after arriving in my spot, the sun finally makes an appearance and, wow, is it worth the wait! Blinding shards of light spring forth through the trees and its warmth on my face is most welcome in the cold of that January morning.

It was by sitting in that field, on that January morning, waiting for the sun to appear, sitting through three stages of twilight, which I had yet to know had names, that I realised how little I knew of its habits and rhythms. So, once I was home in the warmth of my own living room, I started to learn.

In order to understand our ancestors' connections, lore and stories of the sun it is helpful to know a little of the science, so humour me a moment and let's delve into the heliophysics of our life-giving star.

The sun is a yellow dwarf star that is 4.5 billion years old. It is 26,000 light-years away from the galactic centre and is 150 million kilometres from earth. Its core temperature is 15 million °C or 27 million °F. It is the sun's gravity that stops the planets flying around the solar system getting swallowed up by black holes like a giant game of Hungry Hippos. The sun is master of the seasons, ocean currents, climate, radiation, auroras and, of course, the weather. Without the sun we would not survive.

The sun is approximately halfway through its life and according to scientists we have around another 5 billion years left before our star expands and consumes the solar system. That is, of course, unless we end it first.

The route the sun takes across the sky each year is called an analemma. Technically, it's our route, not the sun's, and it's not the sun coming up, it's us tilting at the sun like Don Quixote tilted at windmills. But let's go back to that analemma. There are scientists and photographers who have plotted the position of the sun throughout the year by using complex technology or patiently and painstakingly taking photos in the same spot every week for fifty-two weeks of the year. When they have overlaid these points or photographs, it has essentially created a figure of eight in the sky. This figure of eight has a small loop at the top and a larger loop at the bottom and sits diagonally across the sky. During the shorter loop the sun appears higher in the sky, and during the longer loop the sun appears lower, thus dictating the hours of sunlight we have. During the shorter and higher loop, the sun takes longer to make its journey across the sky each day. This is the summer. The lower and larger loop means the sun is not in the sky for as long. This is winter. It is because of the earth's position and its route around the sun that we get this analemma.

The earth's route around the sun and the angle at which it is tilted results in the seasons, and because of this, the seasons are different in the southern and northern hemispheres. It takes 365¼ days for the earth to move around the sun, and as it does so, different hemispheres are exposed to more or less light.

When the southern hemisphere is tilted towards the sun and the northern away from it, it is winter in the northern hemisphere and summer in the southern. When the northern hemisphere is tilted towards the sun and the southern away, it is summer in the northern hemisphere and winter in the southern. Hence Australians enjoy their Christmas celebrations on the beach and here in the UK we typically enjoy it around the table bingeing on carbohydrates, sugar and grease to get us through the cold weather.

Homo sapiens have been on the earth for around 300,000 years, and for at least 12,000 of those, our ancestors have tracked the path of the sun, knowing with every fibre of their being that the sun plays a major part in providing us with food, warmth and, well, life! Evidence of this tracking of the sun is apparent in monuments across the world and I will explore some of these throughout this book.

You might think it's fairly easy to predict where the sun comes up: the east, right? Well, actually it changes and this is the very problem I had that morning. I was indeed facing east, but I was not looking to the right of me, so south-east, where the winter sun would emerge. As a general rule, in the UK winter months, December to February, the sun rises in the south-east, then from March to May it rises in the east, from June to August in the north-east, then from September to November in the east again. Our ancestors would have had to watch the sun and work out exactly where it would rise in order to illuminate the monuments, megaliths and mountains that became their sacred places during the summer and winter solstices.

As we tilt and spin our way around the sun, the seasons unfurl: winter, spring, summer, autumn. Each cycle marks a year in our calendar, and whilst we know now that the seasons are the result of our planet's tilt and relative position to the sun, this was not always the case for our ancestors.

Many cultures have stories that explain the seasons. The most famous of these in the northern hemisphere is arguably the Greek myth of Persephone. Persephone was the daughter of Demeter, the goddess of the harvest. Whilst wandering in a wildflower meadow, Persephone is stolen. Hades, ruler of the Underworld, hides her deep beneath the earth. The grief of Demeter, mourning for the loss of her daughter, is so great that the fields and plants stop growing.

To right the balance and stop the world from starving, the gods demand that Hades returns Persephone to her mother. There is just one condition: Persephone must not have eaten anything within the realm of Hades. So it is that, before she is released, Hades tricks Persephone into eating six pomegranate seeds whilst she is still in the Underworld. This results in Persephone only being able to return to the surface for six months of each year. During this time the light returns to the world and the fields flourish. When she is forced to return for six months in the Underworld, Demeter again mourns and nothing grows in the fields. For the ancient Greeks, this explained the seasons of summer and winter.

A similar story appears in Native American culture. The Blue Corn Maiden of the Pueblos people is the most desirable of all the corn maidens and so Winter Katsina comes down from the hills and steals her away. The Blue Corn Maiden misses her people and eventually manages to escape her frozen home in the mountains to collect enough Yucca leaves to make a fire to warm herself by. When she does this, Summer Katsina sees her and seeks to rescue her. When Winter Katsina returns from his travels in the mountains and finds Summer Katsina in his house, he is furious and battles him, but the fire of Summer Katsina is too strong and he melts Winter Katsina's weapons of ice. Winter Katsina calls a truce and Summer Katsina returns the Blue Corn Maiden to the Pueblos people. But to keep the peace and stop Winter Katsina blowing snow and ice throughout the lands all year, every six months the Blue Corn Maiden returns to his house in the mountains, to live with Winter Katsina.

Some folktales tell of the months themselves as characters. One such story is a Slovak folktale of a young girl who is sent out into the winter woods by her cruel mother and sister, to find unseasonal flowers and fruit. She finds a circle of women in the forest who turn out to be the twelve months and they are able to provide her with the items she needs, despite it being the depths of winter. In other cases, it is a variety of different deities that are responsible for the different seasons or weather events.

Some myths explain not necessarily the seasons, but why the sun is in a certain position at a certain time of year. In the Hawaiian myth of how Māui slowed down the sun, the story is told of how a long time ago the sun, whose name was Tamanuiterā, travelled too quickly across the sky and the days were too short. As a result, Māui and his brothers had to work hard to get everything done that they needed to in the daylight. One day they became so fed up with this that Māui claimed that he would catch Tamanuiterā and teach him to slow down. Through cunning, team work and brute strength the brothers achieved this, and Tamanuiterā was so tired after struggling to get free that he no longer had the energy to travel so fast across the sky.

The Nart Sagas are a collection of stories from the ancient indigenous ethnic groups of the North Caucasus. These include the Circassians, Abazas, Abkhaz and Ubykhs, which became part of Russia in the late eighteenth century after the Russo-Circassian War.

During this time genocide was employed by the invading forces to gain control over the lands, and as a result much of the ancient traditions and myths of the Caucasus peoples was lost. Various scholars have subsequently translated the Nart Sagas and I first discovered the following story in a collection translated by John Colarusso. It gives a very ancient explanation as to the position of the sun at sunset.

It is important to remember that ancient and indigenous stories should be told with the care and respect they deserve. Whilst many of those translating the stories have sought first-hand accounts and knowledge of the culture from which the tales come, most translations of these tales are not written by those from this culture. This, coupled with the many changes that have occurred in this region over hundreds of years, means that these stories have inevitably been interpreted from the viewpoint of the translator and, in some cases perhaps, changed from their original forms, if only very subtly.

These influences aren't always modern either. For example, Patricia Monaghan cites in her *Encyclopaedia of Goddesses and Heroines* that in the case of south-eastern Europe, as far back as the third century, there may have been outside influences at play in the telling and recording of these stories.

Below is my interpretation of this tale based on my research into these stories and the culture they have come from.

WHY THE SUN PAUSES AT SUNSET

Setenaya was a powerful goddess, a seer and the keeper of an apple tree, which could gift you health and immortality. Setenaya was a bewitching and strong-willed, life-giving woman. Her husband Warzameg would tell you she was a trickster and a wise woman, for she and he lived many a tale and Setenaya had many lessons to impart.

This tale is from long ago, in a time when Setenaya was renowned for her skills as a seamstress and weaver. One day she set herself the task of sewing a saya – a dress that used many metres of fabric and had to be sewn with the utmost care.

A young leatherworker overheard Setenaya set herself this challenge. He proclaimed that he would craft a saddle and that he too would complete it within the day.

The challenge proclaimed, they both set to work on their tasks as the sun began its ascent into the sky from behind the Caucasus Mountains.

The boy, despite his youth, worked expertly with the tanned hide, to cut, stretch and mould it over the wooden saddle tree.

Setenaya wove her fabric with deft hands, until she had enough to cut out the pieces for her dress, experience negating the need for her to measure.

With the sun almost at its zenith, Setenaya sat by the door of her house and began to sew. She held the fabric firm in her thumb and forefinger as her needle moved in and out of the cloth in tiny, neat, uniform stiches, the like of which no other could sew. Head down, she sewed and listened to the gentle hammering of the boy's leatherwork as he tapped it into shape across the saddle tree.

The sun moved across the sky as they both worked on their creations. It watched as the boy wiped the sweat from his forehead and Setenaya unravelled her scarf, which had once kept away the morning's chill.

As the sun began its descending arc, the boy started to etch carvings into the leather of the saddle and Setenaya began to hem her metres of fabric.

The boy finished as the sun was almost touching the horizon, and when Setenaya could no longer hear the music of his work, she looked up. She saw him, feet up and watching the sun as it threatened to turn the sky pink and orange.

Setenaya looked across to the sun and called to it, 'If only you would pause a moment.'

The sun looked up from the horizon and saw Setenaya's sewing. The light caught the delicate fabric of the dress and the perfect stitches, which were not yet quite finished. It looked across at the delightful saddle, polished and shining in the last of its rays, and it did indeed pause for a moment. It waited and watched as Setenaya sewed, watching each stitch as it was completed until finally Setenaya's saya was complete. She held it up for the boy to see and then pulled it over her head.

'See,' she said, 'it took me but a day.'

The boy did not argue, for the sun was indeed still above the horizon.

'You are every bit as magnificent as they say,' replied the boy, smiling at Setenaya.

It is said that from that day on the sun stops on the horizon every day. Perhaps it is to look upon the day's creations, as it once did on Setenaya's.

SUN SALUTATION

In this month's chapter we have (very briefly) explored the science, rhythms and seasons of the sun. We still have many rituals that connect us to the start of the day and the return of the sun. This could be as simple as breakfast, the meal that breaks our nightly fast. A fabulous way to connect daily with the sun is a sequence of yoga poses known as a sun salutation.

Yoga comes from the Sanskrit word *yuj*, which is a root word that means to connect or unite something. The traditions held within yoga were passed down through the generations orally. They were first recorded in the third century in the Rigveda, a Sanskrit script containing hymns, which is one of four volumes known as the Vedas.

In the Hindu faith Lord Shiva, one of the primary gods in the pantheon and one of a trinity with Brahma and Vishnu, was the first to teach the practice of yoga.

Several centuries later, in the mid-nineteenth century, yoga arrived in the west with Swami Vivekananda, a progressive Hindu monk from India who was also an author and philosopher.

Sūryanamaskāra, which translates as 'sun salutation', is one of the best-known sequences in the practice of yoga. Today for many it has become an excellent way of warming up the muscles before exercise. For others it is a deeply spiritual practice. Whether this salutation is referring literally to the sun, or perhaps to a fire within ourselves, is a subject that has been discussed by yoga experts worldwide. As we will discover as we progress through this book, all cultures have in some way or another celebrated and worshipped the sun, so it is possible that this sequence of movements is intended to do just that: worship the sun that holds a link between the light and the dark, or the world of the human and that of the gods.

It could also be linked to the many stories that use fire to represent the uncontrolled passion that lies within us in the form of lust or anger. By performing this sequence of movements, we are keeping that fire in check, and giving it the time and respect it needs in order to do this.

Whatever your beliefs, the practice of yoga and the sun salutation can be a great way of gently getting the circulation going first thing in the morning, calming your mind ready for the day ahead and connecting with the warmth of the sun, even on the coldest of winter days.

As you rise each morning, you could make the sun salutation part of your routine. Find a space that has room for you to stretch out your arms and legs, and is quiet, warm and safe. If you start this exercise in the winter, you could try facing south-east so that you are greeting the sun as it rises.

Below is the sequence of movements that make up the sun salutation. Do remember to listen to your body and only do what you are comfortable with. If you have any injuries or health conditions that may impact on this exercise, you might want to discuss this with your doctor or physiotherapist before trying out the exercise.

If you have never done yoga before, it is recommended that you seek out a yoga expert to get you started. If you would like to see the exercises performed by a yogi online, there are some examples on the website page that accompanies this book. You will find the web address in the introduction.

Sequence of Movements in the Sun Salutation

Remember: one of the overriding principles of yoga is control, so each of these movements should be transitioned between, slowly and smoothly, with care and mindfulness.

Begin in Mountain Pose – Tadasana.
Gradually move to Forward Fold – Uttanasana.
Slowly move up to Half Lift – Ardha Uttanasana.
Move back to Forward Fold – Uttanasana.
Step back into Downward-Facing Dog – Adho Mukha Svanasana.
Come down onto your knees and lower your body down to the floor through your arms, moving into Cobra – Bhujangasana.
Lower yourself back to the floor, then tuck your toes under and lift back to Downward-Facing Dog – Adho Mukha Svanasana.
Walk your feet back towards your hands and into Forward Fold once more – Uttanasana.
Then slowly rise to Half Lift – Ardha Uttanasana.
Move back to Forward Fold – Uttanasana.
Stand up slowly to Mountain Pose – Tadasana.
Finish with the palms of your hands together and held over the heart – Añjali Mudrā.

FEBRUARY

THE IN-BETWEEN

I AM UP AT SIX again and out at twenty past the hour. Security lights fling themselves on, but as I walk along the street, I can see well without them. Although I'm out at the same time as I was in January, the difference in the light level is tangible. This is the beginning of the civil twilight.

There are three phases of twilight before the sunrise and these are astronomical twilight, nautical twilight and civil twilight. These twilights are defined by the angle at which the earth is to the sun. Yes, yet again it's all to do with the angle at which we are tilted. As we turn further towards the sun, the light grows through the three twilights until sunrise and the transition between night and day is complete.

Civil twilight is the brightest of the three and the time when it is considered that human eyes can see to complete most tasks, even though the sun is not yet above the horizon. The further north or south from the equator you are, the longer the twilight; hence the midnight sun that occurs in the far north of Scandinavia and at the poles. Civil twilight, unless you live close to or along the equator, is generally longer in the summer. In January I sat through all three of these twilights immersed in the crepuscular spaces of the in-between.

At the end of the street, framed by the rooftops, a soft orange glow offers the promise of the day. Most of the songbirds are not yet up and the solo voice of a crow calls indignantly at the cold wind.

I pass the deserted local pub, abandoned village hall, houses still in darkness punctuated by the percussive lights from house and car alarms, until I reach the red glow of a lonely temporary traffic light, which, sensing my presence, greets me at the junction with an amber and a green.

The first songbird I hear is the blackbird. I cross the road and start to walk up the hill, along the path corridored by the still-bare tree branches above. Pigeons clap, a passive aggressive audience politely adhering to convention, but they can't get out of there quick enough.

Soon the path leaves the gardens and houses behind and crepuscular light hugs me tight as the winter wind snatches at my hair and rattles the tree branches above me. I am reminded of the story of 'The Travelling Tree', a tale collected by Ruth Tongue in her book *Forgotten Folk-Tales of the English Counties.*

It's the tale of a man who, when he has to visit a sick relative, discovers he has to travel far into the dead of night in the most atrocious weather. To cut a short story even shorter, when he finds a tree to shelter under, the tree does not stay still as he expects. Instead, the tree leans in and tells him that it does not know what his plans might be on such a terrible night, but that it is running off home, and the tree promptly disappears into the night. Perhaps these trees, too, are leaning in to ask me what on earth I am doing at such an hour on a Sunday morning.

I know this path well from daytime strolls, but as the branches become denser overhead, the light plays tricks on me and I struggle to see where it is safe to put my feet amongst the roots and rabbit holes.

February is surely the coldest month and I am again grateful for my fleece-lined ski trousers. These are accompanied by thick walking socks, a down jacket and three polo necks, yes three. According to the weather forecast it is 4°C, but with a friendly little reminder that it will feel like –1°C. I can bear witness to this. The wind is bitter.

I pause by the frozen water trough, next to the gate to the field. The branches that fell into it at the end of last year are now jet black, suspended in the ice.

I follow the edge of the wood to my sit-spot and watch as the perfect printer-cartridge sky begins its sunrise kaleidoscope through magenta, yellow and cyan.

The wind is too high for me to hear the songbirds well, but the local rooks are clearly audible above the hurly burly of the 30mph gusts of wind.

From where I am sitting, I can see the temporary traffic light in the village cycling through its colours: red, orange, green, orange, red, summoning the traffic.

It is barren in February up on the hill and, with the wind taking all the usual sounds of life with it, I feel quite alone.

This time last month I could hear at least a smattering of songbirds singing in the trees behind me, but this morning it is the wind that shouts in my ears. It distorts the usual voices of nature and a startled pheasant makes me jump as the wind whips it into more of a shriek than an echoing cluck.

The crepuscular creatures I share this space with do not usually spook me. I recognise their calls, but this morning feels different. Wilder. Less predictable. Darker. The fox, tawny owl, deer, hares, badgers and bats all have the upper hand when it comes to seeing and hearing clearly in the gloaming of a February morning.

Some of these creatures will become regular visitors on the hill, whom I will get to know as I progress through the year with my sunrise vigils. One of them is a rather vocal deer.

The first time it appeared, it was just a head above a ridge-line in the field where I was sitting. The ridge is perhaps a lynchet caused by years of farming and it slightly obscures my view of the horse jumps further down the slope. It must act in the same way for anything walking towards where I am sitting, as the deer came from that direction. It barked, ducked down, put its head back up and barked again. This continued for around five minutes until it bounded grace-fully across the meadow and back into the woods, where it continued to bark for a while.

I had not encountered this behaviour before and, from what I could see, I was not in its path and there were unlikely to be any young deer in the grass anywhere near me, as it was far too early for fawns.

The bark of a roe deer is a very distinctive sound and can be quite disconcerting if you don't know what it is, or more to the point what it means. In the case of the roe deer that visits me on the hill, I am still not absolutely sure if it is barking a warning to others, telling me I had better get out of the way, or is just curious. It has on occasion looked like it's about to run at me, at which point I have stood up and shown it that I am not up for wrestling. Yet these encounters persist, which makes them most likely an assertion of territory on its part; after all, I am effectively sitting in its living room having a coffee. I have no right to this spot and so it wishes to challenge that. I can see its point of view, but if I could only speak deer, I would assure it that I am just here for the sunrise and that it is very welcome to come and sit and watch the sun come up with me, even share my coffee, although, on reflection, a roe buck high on caffeine might not be such a good idea.

Thankfully we have never come to blows and we have since reached an agreement of sorts, which goes something like this. You bark at me. I'll stay here and look nonchalant. You eventually get bored. Everyone's happy.

I might have a different opinion on this matter should I be faced with a red deer stag, which can weigh up to around 200kg, but this is a roe buck and the heaviest it's likely to be is around 25kg – much more manageable, although I still wouldn't want to test it.

When I did some research around deer behaviour of this kind, I discovered that a naturalist named Frances Pitt had recorded a similar encounter in her book *Wild Animals in Britain*, published in 1944. She was walking in Scotland and had sat beneath a tree, drifted off to sleep and was dreaming about a dog, when she awoke to find that a male roe deer was the source of the barking, not a dog. She describes the deer as looking as if it were both surprised and alarmed by her presence. A little like my roe buck of the South Downs, no doubt, yet almost eighty years on from Pitt's recordings.

Roe deer are native to the UK and there is evidence that our Palaeolithic ancestors would have lived in a landscape that included the roe deer. It's no real wonder, then, that it's made its way into our heritage and history.

The image of the deer has appeared in many Palaeolithic cave paintings, such as the black stag in Lascaux caves in south-west France. Our ancestors relied heavily on the deer for its meat, skin and antlers. Antlers could be shaped into harpoons to fish with, picks for mining and handles for tools.

Often, because these tools were needed in large supply, especially when mining, the deer were carefully managed and their antlers harvested as they shed them. Our spoken legend and mythology carried the deer and stag forward with us and these stories often morphed these very real beings into horned gods.

The deer in this form was worshipped in many cultures, and headdresses were created from the skull and antlers of the deer. When worn by a hunter it would allow them to become half-human, half-deer and enter the mind of their quarry.

A headdress of this kind, made from part of a skull and antlers of a deer, was found in the grave of a Mesolithic woman in North Yorkshire, more famously known as the Star Carr woman. It is thought that she would have been a shaman of some kind, tapping into the magic of the deer in order to aid the community. At Star Carr several of these headdresses, known in archaeological terms as frontlets, were found. They are now on display in the Yorkshire Museum in York, England.

As people began to record human knowledge of the natural world, the medieval bestiaries noted that deer had certain mythical and magical properties. Richard Barber's translation of the MS Bodley 764 thirteenth-century Medieval Bestiary notes that, if a deer is unwell, it will lure a snake out of the undergrowth, breath on it to neutralise the venom and eat it. It was also thought that deer carried the secret to eternal youth as the Bestiary notes that after eating the aforementioned snake, the deer would go and drink from a fresh spring and become rejuvenated.

The illuminated manuscript goes on to say how the sound of panpipe music will mesmerise deer and that they will run with the wind if they hear dogs so that their scent is carried away with them – which, unlike the snake hypotheses, is closer to the truth. Perhaps with this in mind I should take some pan pipes with me to my sit-spot next time?

As you might expect, throughout history the stag has lent itself to our culture as a very masculine symbol. Stags often represent strength and fertility, wildness and mystery. The shedding and regrowth of horns could be seen as emblematic of the circle of life and rebirth. They are further connected with creation through mythologies such as the Norse creation myth. In this myth, four stags named Dáinn, Dvalinn, Duneyrr and Duraþrór can be found nibbling at the leaves, flowers and branches of Yggdrasil, the world tree. These four stags are thought to represent the four winds and perhaps the passage of time.

Stags and deer often crop up in creation stories from northern Europe, and in Sámi mythology, the goddess of the sun is Beaivi and each year a white reindeer is sacrificed in her name in order to ensure the return of the summer.

Hinds represent a softer side to the deer's nature. Several of the Greek goddesses are associated with hinds. Artemis is the most notable, as the goddess of the hunt.

The Golden Hind of Greek myth was sacred to Artemis. This hind was also known as the Ceryneian hind and is a chaste hind with golden antlers and hooves. In some myths, Artemis has four of these Ceryneian hinds to pull her chariot. It is said that she found five of them but that she allowed the fifth to remain free so as to serve as one of the labours of Hercules. The image of Artemis' deer-drawn chariot is mirrored in Celtic mythology with Flidais the goddess of the woodland, who also has a chariot drawn by deer.

In Celtic folklore, the stag belongs to the fairy folk and this is very clearly evident in many stories told of them, and even in modern-day interpretations of these folk. Look no further than the image of Thranduil, the elk-riding elven king, in the film franchise of Tolkien's *The Hobbit* and *The Lord of the Rings*. Well before Tolkien, this mythology had gained deer the nickname of 'Fairy Cattle' in the Highlands of Scotland.

In the Celtic pantheon, there are many gods and goddesses associated with deer. Two examples are Flidais, as previously mentioned, and Elen of the Ways, another forest-protecting goddess who it is thought was once a real person. Possibly the most ancient of these deities is the horned god. He is depicted as a stag, goat, bull or ram depending on where you are in Britain. His image is usually naked and he sometimes appears with a serpent that has a ram's head, again linking deer and stags to snakes. He also wears a heavy necklace known as a torque.

Like the stag, this god represents fertility and strength and is seen as a warrior. One of the most famous depictions of the horned god is on the inside of the Gundestrup Cauldron, which dates from the first century BCE. It was discovered in Jutland, Denmark and currently resides in the National Museum of Denmark in Copenhagen.

This horned god is often given the name Cernunnos. He is the ruler of beasts, protector of the forest and god of plenty. In his human form he is seen with stag antlers rising from his head. He is also the Celtic god of the underworld, who also occasionally appears with a serpent that has the head of a ram and a torque around his neck, so it is often assumed that the horned god and Cernunnos are one and the same. He was thought mainly to have been worshipped in Britain but when the Christian Church started to gain popularity, he became demonised. His name can be seen to be derived from the Gaulish word *karnon*, meaning horn or antler.

Whilst the deer and their associated gods and goddesses roam in the half-light, so too do the gods and goddess that are associated with the dark half of the year, light and the return of the sun.

The Cailleach (kall-i-ac) is an ancient hag goddess also found in Celtic lore and she is associated not only with deer but also with the cycle of life and the returning of the light. She is said to walk the earth half the year, between the Samhain on 31 October and the Beltane on 30 April. Whilst she is most prevalent in Celtic mythology and lore, she can be found in various forms across Europe in myth, legend and folklore.

As the image of the Cailleach is so prolific and she has become so many things, she occasionally blurs into other mythological and folkloric beings. One of these is the Glaistig, a half-woman, half-goat akin to a satyr. Glaistigs are green maidens and there is a legend of a Glaistig that was found mourning the loss of the Caledonian forest by striking two deer shanks together. To come full cycle, this story is also mirrored in the story of 'The Cailleach and the Deer Hunter'.

In February we reach the Imbolc (ee-molc). This is the halfway point between the winter solstice and the vernal equinox and takes place around 1 February. It is said that if the sun is shining on this day then the Cailleach has brought this to pass because she wishes to collect more wood for her fire. The good weather will allow her to extend the winter and so, as a consequence, we have many more cold days ahead of us. If, however, it is cold and dark on this day then the Cailleach is away indoors beside the fire with no stomach for the winter and will let the light return early.

Furthermore, this connection with the light and the sun is represented in the belief that the Cailleach is the daughter of Grainne, goddess of the sun. Grainne is also sometimes associated with Aine, goddess of the summer. There are many stories of Grainne in Irish mythology and in some she is the winter sun to her sister Aine's summer sun. These two goddesses are also referred to as Sidhe (shee), which are the Irish fairy folk.

Back on the hill I sit waiting for the sun to rise; a glorious dark-pink sky covers the horizon. It lights up the clouds, creating a mackerel sky akin to a crazy 1980s Artex ceiling for the world. This time I've brought buttered malt loaf for breakfast and I pour myself a coffee and wait.

The pink sky grows in its intensity and now there is an accompanying orange glow like a fluorescent light becoming brighter and brighter until it echoes the industrial orange of the indicator lights waiting patiently at the junction in the valley. As the sun starts to rise, it pushes the other colours out of the sky, washing it out with its rays, giving way to the blue of the day.

Shafts of light burst forth and rain down on the earth. I can feel the sun's power as its vibrations warm the ground. She is Eos, she is Sol, she is Aine, she is here!

Forty minutes later and all that is left is a lemon-yellow glow at the edges of the clouds, which prevent me from soaking up any more of the sun's energy.

In the summer, scientists have found that we need as little as fifteen minutes of sunlight a day in order to get the amount of vitamin D our bodies need to function properly and prevent conditions such as rickets occurring. But in winter, in the northern parts of the UK, the sun's UVB rays that hold this medicine simply do not reach us. And so, we have to rely on our diets to provide us with the rest and get us through the weak-sunned winter.

It is time to head back home to the warmth of the central heating, the kettle and perhaps some fried eggs on toast, sunny side up. As I walk back through the trees, there are signs of life once more. A fluorescent, fuzzy caterpillar abseils from a tree branch above me and I stop to chat with a great tit about the day ahead. I reach the road once more and the traffic light has found the company of morning traffic.

THE CAILLEACH AND THE DEER HUNTER

Cailleach stories are slightly different depending on where in the many Celtic nations they hail from. The bones of the following story are from the Scottish legend of Donald Cameron, a hunter from Lochaber. However, I have taken several snippets of Scottish Cailleach lore and legends to create my own interpretation of the story.

The Cailleach of Caledonia was said to protect the deer. She knew that some would fall to the huntsman, as that is what keeps nature in balance, and so it was the hinds that she protected most fiercely, allowing the stags to provide meat and hides for the community. To keep the hinds safe, she had cast apotropaic magic upon the hinds in the forest behind her hut so that no arrow would pierce their skin and they might look after their young without fear.

Her home was a little hut on the shores of Loch Leven and one spring the Cailleach was preparing to weave a new winter shawl, as she did each year. She had the softest sheep's wool, which she had spent the previous winter combing, spinning and dying with woad, so that it was the same deep glorious blue of the loch.

Donald Cameron too lived beside the loch, yet he had never met the Cailleach. She hid herself from him in all her forms.

Donald was famed for miles around for his skill at hunting. If you needed meat, hide or antler, Donald could provide it. The meat was hung with care, cured and could feed a family well. The hides were stripped, fleshed, salted, cleaned, tanned and broken to perfection, and the antlers were only from the older stags, perfect for tools, handles and drinking horns. The winter had been long and he would need to replenish his stocks soon with the coming of the spring.

It was the last days of February and the Cailleach was bathing in the loch waters whilst the wool she had dyed and washed, ready to begin her shawl, was hung about the lower branches of the pine trees, drying in the sun.

As she bathed, she felt the warmth of the sun on her skin and its rejuvenating effect on her. She closed her eyes and as she did a young hind appeared at the edge of the trees. It saw the blue wool and wondered what delicacy this might be. It pushed the wool with its snout, reached up with a long tongue and nibbled a little.

The Cailleach opened her eyes and she saw the hind taking liberties with her precious wool. She stood up in the loch, water dripping from her glowing skin. She grew taller until a shadow fell on the hind and she proclaimed that it no longer had her protection.

Over the coming spring, the Cailleach wove her shawl and the deer continued to roam in the woods, but none of them dared to approach the Cailleach's house again for fear of her wrath.

That summer Donald was out hunting. The sun was high and it was warm, but he had to stay out until he had made his kill. He had failed to shoot anything yet this week and he needed something to make sure he had enough to see him and the village through the winter.

He spotted a young hind at the edge of the forest. Whilst he had never yet managed to kill a hind on the shores of Loch Leven, he was willing to try, hoping for an easy kill and a light load, so that he might return home quickly and shelter from the heat and midges.

He drew back his bow and let the arrow fly. It arced high and hit true and his luck held. The hind was slain. He carried it back to his house on the opposite side of the loch and began the process of skinning the carcass, hanging the meat and making use of every bit of the animal. The hind meat was succulent and the hide was soft. He would get a pretty penny for this!

Through the summer and into the autumn he hunted, but he never again managed to fell a hind; plenty of young bucks, yes, but not a hind. He hung the skeleton of the hind along the side of his hut as a macabre trophy, and he refused to sell any of the bones to anyone who might enquire. This was his one and only hind.

One evening, as he sat on the porch after a hard day tanning hides and breaking them, he fell asleep in the late afternoon sun. He drifted in and out of a fitful slumber until he awoke to the most beautiful sound.

It was the voice of a woman singing a mournful tune. As he opened his eyes, he saw a woman in her later life, not yet aged as his mother had been when she passed last year, but by no means a young maiden. Her eyes were full of wisdom and held fine lines in the corners. As she sang, she knocked together two deer shanks, and when he looked to the hanging hind skeleton that he so treasured, he saw the shanks were missing.

'They're mine,' he announced and stood up, striding forward to take them from the woman.

With the voice of an old oak tree, the woman looked up, her face wet with tears, and replied, 'They are not, they were hers.' She was waving the shank bones towards the rest of the skeleton.

'She is deed,' Donald said bluntly. 'They no longer serve her.'

'You should not kill the hinds,' the woman replied. 'They hold the next generation.'

'It is my right to hunt,' replied Donald. 'Lord Leven requests it and I will hunt the deer as I see fit – there are plenty of them.'

Donald did not know that he was speaking to the Cailleach of the loch, the protector of the hinds, and what's more, he did not care to find out to whom he spoke. Yes, she was a fine woman, clearly of an age where she should understand the world, but what he hunted was his business and his alone.

'Give me the shanks,' he said, holding out his hand, palm up.

'Very well,' replied the woman, 'but you will never hunt again on the shores of this loch.'

She placed the shanks in his hand and, as she did, he looked into her soft, brown doe eyes, weary with the years. He heard the singing once more, this time ringing in his ears, yet she made no sound. He felt his body tense and his arms ache. He could barely lift the shanks, never mind his legs that were now lead-heavy, and he struggled to place one foot in front of the other as he returned to the house.

He crawled the last few feet into his bed as mist swept across the loch encircling the house. The singing did not leave his ears. As he closed his eyes, he could see the image of the hind, this time with the wild woman's eyes, and he fell into a deep sleep.

When Donald did not appear at the usual markets with the venison, tanned hides and bone ware that the villagers required, they started to worry. A man from the community was sent up to the loch to see what had happened to Donald. He found him in his bed in a torpor. He could not wake him and yet he could see the rise and fall of his chest and flickering of his eyelids as he dreamed.

The man went to seek the advice of the wise woman, Old Biddy, and she too visited Donald. She saw his sleeping form and she saw the two deer shanks still clutched in his hands, tight to his chest.

'This is the Cailleach's doing,' she said. 'There is nothing we can do for Donald now. He hunted one too many deer. Do not undo it for it will have grave consequences for all.'

The villagers heeded Biddy at first, but when Donald slept for the whole winter, that did not suit the villagers at all for Donald was their best hunter. They had eaten through their supplies of meat and their shoes were worn from the ice and snow.

No one knew how long it would be before someone else arrived in the village who was even half as good as Donald. There would be less meat without Donald, a lack of hides for beds and shoes, coats and boots. Soon a group of villagers visited the castle and Lord Leven came to know of what had befallen his best hunter and that Old Biddy would not help, so he took matters into his own hands.

He sent an emissary to the apothecary in the village, a man of renown who claimed to have a cure for everything.

The emissary told the whole tale to the apothecary and as the apothecary listened, he considered.

'What did Biddy say?' asked the apothecary.

'That there was nothing we could do,' replied the emissary.

'Then you'd best heed her,' replied the apothecary.

'But we can't leave poor Donald like that, plus what will we do for shoes?' came the reply.

'There's other meat and other hides,' the apothecary replied stubbornly. He knew that if Biddy wouldn't tell them what to do, there was a good reason for it.

'You must know,' pressed the emissary.

The apothecary shook his head.

'There's gold in it, for ye,' smiled the emissary. Lord Leven had been quite clear that he wanted his best hunter well and working again, regardless of the cost.

As it happened, the apothecary had not been as profitable as he would have liked over the summer. Biddy had taken a lot of his work as the hedgerows had been plentiful and she had been teaching the villagers how to find their own cures.

'Very well,' replied the apothecary, 'I'll see what my books have to say. Deer shanks in his hand, you say?'

The emissary nodded.

The apothecary lifted down a large, dusty tome and searched through the index until he found what he was looking for. C for Cailleach. He read, took in the information, looked up at the emissary and raised an index finger.

'Now listen here,' he said. 'You haven't got long. This is a Cailleach's curse; the only way to lift it is by getting rid of the Cailleach that resides at Loch Leven. Each February at the beginning of the month, she will emerge and bathe herself in the loch. An old woman enters the loch and a young maiden emerges from it. Both are the Cailleach and in this way she has immortality, but there is a way to rid yourself of her. Take your best sheepdog up there and wait, all the rest of the month of January if you have to. When you see her enter the lake, and you will for she cannot disguise herself at this point, make sure the dog barks. This will break her concentration; she will not be able to complete the transformation and she will fade away into the loch. When she is gone, the curse will be lifted and Donald will wake.'

The emissary returned to the lord and told him what the apothecary had found. He was given one of the finest hunting dogs, and in the last dark days of January the emissary headed out to Donald's hut by the loch.

He had been there almost a week when a muted light seeped in through the windows of the hut. A mist still surrounded the loch and he could only just see the shape of a figure standing on the opposite side of the water. This must be her. He moved slowly out of the hut, indicating to the dog to stay quiet, and he crept down to the edge of the loch and waited and watched, watched and waited.

The figure was bent low and limped, tentatively finding her footing on the shingle beside the loch, a blue shawl pulled tight around her. She moved further into the water until it was up to her middle and finally her shoulders. Now she closed her eyes and leaned back into the water, floating, her silver hair spilling out around her face like bleached seaweed, mixing with the mist that clung to the surface of the loch.

The emissary knew this was his chance. He lifted his foot and kicked the dog, which yelped and barked, cowering from an unjust boot. The dog's bark rang out over the loch and the Cailleach opened her eyes as the sun pushed through the mist. She melted into the loch, a Cailleach no more.

Inside the hut Donald awoke with a raging hunger in his belly and an ache in every muscle. He sat up on the edge of his bed, testing to see if his legs would work. Pushing up through his hands, he found they did not. They were numb with sleep. As he was attempting to rub some life back into his aching limbs, Lord Leven's emissary came back through the door of the hut, the dog slinking in behind him.

'You're awake!' he proclaimed, grinning from ear to ear. 'Lord Leven will be pleased – you have been asleep for three months.'

Donald looked at him confused. 'Three months?' he asked incredulously.

'Sit there. I'll get ye fud and explain.' The emissary produced food from the kitchen and told his story as Donald ate Bannock breads, porridge and salted venison. When he was full of food and story, he began to gain a little of his strength.

'A Cailleach, you say?' he asked the emissary. 'And was it Biddy who told you how to cure me?'

'No, she wadna help. It was the apothecary.'

Donald drew in a deep breath. 'Then no good will come of it,' he said, for Donald knew that the Cailleach was the linchpin in the cycle of life.

The days became weeks, the weeks became months and Donald regained his strength and health, but he never hunted again. Lord Leven tried everything he could to persuade him, even threatened him with the noose on some trumped-up treason charge if he did not return to hunting, but Donald was not moved and Lord Leven did not follow through with his threats.

Donald continued to live out his days in the hut on the loch, and if he has not died of old age then he is still there now, watching and waiting for the return of the Cailleach. For he knows that when she returns a natural order to things will be restored, the cycle of life will be in balance again. For he took what was not his and if he is not allowed to pay the price of his mistake, well then, we shall all have to.

WEAVING THE SUN

Creation is a strong theme that runs through the Cailleach myths and legends. Connected with the theme of creations and cycles is the act of weaving, and that is why in my interpretation of the Cailleach's story she weaves herself a new shawl, each year.

In many mythologies from east to west, there are weaving gods and goddesses, predominately associated with fate and creation but also with the sky. Many weave the stars but several also weave the sun. In Norse mythology it is sometimes noted that Sol was a weaver, using the sun as her spindle and the sun rays her yarn.

In Greek mythology, Arachne who challenged Athena to a weaving competition, much to her own detriment, is in some versions of the myths the granddaughter of the sun god. There have also been grave finds dated to the Roman period of amber spindles, perhaps again linking weaving with the sun.

For this chapter's activity I am inviting you to embroider the sun. I have included deer antlers in the design, as a symbol of the winter and the cycle of life that is contained in the Cailleach story you have just read. You might choose either to embroider the sun alone, or include the antlers in your design. You can download the design, and find handy how-tos and suggested embroidery suppliers, via the website page that accompanies this book. You will find the web address in the introduction.

Deer and the Winter Sun Embroidery

What You Will Need

I recommend using Anchor or DMC threads, which are good-quality threads and lovely to sew with. But there are many different makes of thread to choose from, and if you have a favourite, please do use those. Below is a list of the things you will need to complete the full embroidery:

Black cotton fabric at least 25cm × 25cm
15cm wooden embroidery hoop (sometimes you can buy the fabric and hoop together, with the fabric already in the hoop)
Embroidery needle
One skein of gold metallic embroidery thread (suggested DMC E3821)
At least two skeins of embroidery thread in two different shades of yellow (suggested DMC 729 and 743)
One skein of fawn-coloured embroidery thread (suggested DMC 07)
Seed beads (optional)
White carbon paper
Printout of the pattern available on the website page that accompanies this book. You will find the web address in the introduction.

How to Complete the Embroidery

If you've never embroidered before, don't worry. The stitches I have chosen for this design are very simple and suitable for beginners. You can find stitch tutorials via the web address in the introduction.

First, you will need to place the black cloth in the embroidery hoop. Catch the cloth in-between the two parts of the hoop and ensure it is pulled tight and centred.

Next, trace the downloaded design onto the white carbon paper and then transfer it onto your piece of black cotton cloth. You will need to match up the centre of the design and the centre of the black cloth to ensure the design will fit within the frame.

Start with the outline of the antlers. Each piece of embroidery thread is usually made up of six strands. Cut a length of the fawn thread, around 40cm, and separate out two strands. Using the two strands together, backstitch around the outline.

If the design rubs off as you are stitching, you can always retrace and transfer it again.

Next, use two strands of your favoured yellow to backstitch around the sun circle and a combination of the yellows and gold to backstitch the rays of the sun.

Once all the backstitch is complete, you should have the outline of your embroidery.

You can now go back and fill in your deer antlers with satin stitch. This is an easy stitch to fill large areas of a design. Use three strands of the fawn-coloured thread again around 40cm long. Stitch diagonally in-between the different parts of the antler from one line of backstitch to the one opposite, making sure the lines of thread are as close together as possible, as if you are colouring in your antlers with the thread.

Once you have filled in the antlers, use a small running stitch to create rows of stitches in a spiral circling the sun. Use two strands of the thread as you are sewing and alternate shades of yellow each time your thread runs out.

As a final touch, if you have some gold thread left, you could dot some French knots around the sun's ray to add to the design.

To frame your piece, with the embroidery still in the frame, pull it tight across the frame, turn it over and cut off the excess material at the back, leaving a border of around 1 inch. Sew a running stitch around the edge of the fabric and pull tight. Double stitch the end and trim off the excess thread. Your piece is now ready to hang.

MARCH

CLOCK WATCHING

TWO MONTHS AGO, I WAS sitting in my sit-spot in astronomical twilight, near darkness, but now, as the church clock chimes six o'clock, the sun is already on its way up.

As I walked through the village, the golden buds of the daffodils beside the bus stop shone like stars on the verge, and in the field where I now sit, there are a plethora of bright yellow dandelions, which in the words of Vladimir Nabokov will change 'from suns into moons' come May.

In Gaelic, the name for the dandelion is Bearnan Bride, which translates as 'little notched plant of Bride'. Bride or Brigid is a Celtic goddess of fertility, celebrated during Imbolc. It is said that Brigid believed that this plant could provide sustenance for newborn cattle and sheep. More frequently in England, the seed heads of the dandelion are referred to as a clock.

This name for the dandelion seed head is thought to be linked to a children's game where you blow on the seed head in order to tell what the time is. If it takes you three breaths to blow all the seeds away, it's three o'clock. It isn't terribly scientific but no doubt provides entertainment and can literally while away the hours for small children.

Prompted by the dandelions, I consider the concept of time further. There are two events this month that relate to the passing of time: the equinox, occurring around 21 March, when day and night are almost equal, and the very human construct that is daylight savings.

Our modern cities and towns need the measurement of time in order to function, but even before commerce and industry, the agricultural world structured its working days around the hours of light available to it.

Today, many parts of the world adjust the clocks to allow them to make the most of the natural lengthening of daylight hours in the summer, just as the farmers adjusted their day. This is referred to as daylight saving and involves moving the clocks an hour forward. The time is then moved back again in the winter.

Aside from a period of time during the Second World War, when a similar daylight-saving scheme was introduced to preserve energy, the idea of daylight saving wasn't instigated officially in the UK until the British Summer Time Act of 1972.

As the 5,000-year-old megaliths of Europe stand to testify, our ancestors most likely observed the two solstices of the year: the Summer Solstice, which marks the longest day, and the Winter Solstice, which marks the longest night. There is evidence to suggest that they would also have marked the midway points between these solstices. They would have seen that the two equinoxes, vernal and autumnal, were when the period of daylight and the period of darkness were pretty much equal. It is the vernal equinox as I sit here in my usual spot, awaiting the sun's arrival. One of the points on our original, solar clock.

So, when did we start to create a structure for time?

Humans have always measured time in simple terms: day and night. The myth of Horus is evidence of humans acknowledging this. In Egyptian mythology, Horus is a falcon god whose eyes represent the sun and the moon; the right being the sun and the left the moon. Horus is also closely related to the kings of Egypt, who were seen as keepers of the sun, but I will go into this in more detail a little later. For now, I'd like to stick with the concept of time.

Day and night are obvious and tangible ideas. There were times when our ancestors were able to see to do tasks, hunt and continue with daily life, and then other times when they could not see so well and were vulnerable to predators. In this way, the concept of day and night would have been vital for survival. It's part of our circadian rhythms and, like breathing, it would have required little thought. It's natural.

The past, the present and the future would also have been evident to our ancestors. There is a today, there was a yesterday and hopefully there will be a tomorrow. Again, our mythologies bear witness to this with, for example, the weaving Fates of Greek mythology and the spinning Norns of Scandinavian mythology.

So, when did we start sectioning off the hours in the day?

It is thought that the construct of time was created in ancient Egypt around 1500 BCE. The word 'time' possibly evolved from a Proto-Indo-European word *di-mon*, which meant to divide. The first timepieces were sundials. These dials were divided into twelve parts, which varied in size depending on the time of the year. So these were not necessarily uniform hours, as we know them now, but sections of a day.

Of course, this method only measured daylight hours. Methods of measuring the hours of darkness included hourglasses and candles.

The first use of a candle clock was thought to have been recorded by You Jiangu, a sixth-century Chinese poet, who described six candles that had been designed to be the same size and weight. Each candle had twelve sections on it that measured twenty minutes each and four hours in total. All together they could measure the time across a twenty-four-hour period.

The invention of the hourglass is attributed to Liutprand, an eighth-century French monk, although there is no reliable evidence of this. On the subject of monks, however, and moving into the Middle Ages, it was most probably their tradition of ringing bells at various points in the day, to indicate times for devotion and prayer, that eventually spread to the wider community as a way of telling time. The maritime industry then introduced the first accurate clocks in the form of marine chronometers. In this case, the chronometers used the stars to correlate an accurate time.

This use of the stars rather than the sun to measure time can also be seen in the ancient Nebra Sky Disc. The Nebra Sky Disc dates from the Bronze Age. It consists of a round, bronze disc, covered in a malachite green, with gold markings that are thought to represent the sun, moon and stars.

The solstices are also represented in the arrangement of the celestial objects, as well as the seven stars of the constellation Pleiades. So how did this measure time?

The disc was found in a region of eastern Germany and in this region the star constellation of Pleiades can be seen in the sky from early March through to mid-October. It is therefore thought that this was used to mark the beginning and end of the farming year. The solstices were marked with the bands to the left and right sides of the disc, which corresponded to the sunrise and sunset at these times when viewed from the Mittelberg mount in Nebra, Germany. The final curve of gold at the bottom of the disc is considered to have been added later as a depiction of a ship in which the sun could travel across the sky.

Almost 3,000 years later, in the year CE 725, an Anglo-Saxon monk from Northumbria, named Bede, was writing a manuscript entitled *The Reckoning of Time*. In this book, the Venerable Bede looks at how his ancestors measured time and how the Christian calendar was eventually constructed. Bede points out that there are three ways of measuring time: through nature, through custom and through organisations that are in authority – for example, governance or religion.

Time passing within nature can be observed in the seasons and the course of the sun. Customs observe time through our traditions of having seven days in a week or a certain number of days in a month. Governance measures time through holidays for religious holy days (and more recently, daylight saving). Bede goes on to look at many aspects of time and essentially analyses them as constructs. Given that he was a monk, he looks specifically at how time is measured in the Christian religion.

We still base our clocks on the ancient twelve-hour format, only now it has become twenty-four hours and, certainly since the industrial revolution, each one of those hours is tradable and worth something. Time is valuable in our fast-moving society and time is not safe from the notion that it can be used and disposed of. We soak it up, wring it out, use up every last drop, and often complain we don't have enough of it, sometimes without really being conscious of what we actually use it for. By controlling time, it could be argued that we are losing touch with our natural circadian rhythms.

Circadian rhythms are natural rhythms within our DNA that help us to function at our best. In the case of the sun, the light levels during day and night indicate to our brain whether or not we should be awake or asleep. It is a well-known fact that the introduction of synthetic light and light-emitting technology not only allowed us to extend our working day, but also disrupted these circadian rhythms.

The study of these rhythms is known a chronobiology and in 2017 the Nobel prize was awarded to three chronobiologists who had successfully isolated the gene that controls these biological rhythms. Furthermore, they showed that we still very much rely on this inner clock to help us through the day. It was also discovered that if we ignore these rhythms, we are more susceptible to illness and disease, and even the medicines and treatments we use to fight illness and disease may in fact be more effective if taken at particular times of day.

Our ancestors knew you couldn't fight time. The sun would rise and the sun would set and time would move forward. Therefore, they often explained time and fate through the gods and goddesses of their cultures.

In Norse mythology, Mundilfari can be seen to be the god of timekeeping, his name roughly translating as 'he who turns the mill handles'. Hu is the Egyptian god of infinity and/or eternity and you can find him as one of Ra's crew mates in his sky boat. In Egypt, the king was often believed to be the sun itself and as such was responsible for the passage of time by honouring the correct god at the correct time. Stephen Quirke states in his book *The Cult of Ra* that the god Hu (also spelt Huh and Heh) was the god associated with the second hour of the twelve in the Egyptian sundial clocks previously mentioned.

Often the gods of creation hold the key to time and this is so in the case of Balinese god of the underworld, Batara Kāla. In this case Kāla in his name is a Sanskrit word that can mean both time and death, and in this way he becomes associated with the underworld, death and time.

A goddess you will most likely have heard of from the Hindu religion is the powerful and often terrifying Kali who, whilst primarily the goddess of death and destruction, is also sometimes seen as the goddess of time.

The Buddhist god Mahākāla combines the Sanskrit words for 'great' and 'time/death' again. So it is that many, many gods and goddesses find themselves associated with and revered for their hold on time.

The accompanying gods and goddesses of the seasons in each pantheon vary in name and number, but they are all considered to keep the natural order of things and ensure that nature observes the passage of time held by the great deities of life and death.

Time marches on and with it brings fate. Enter the gods and goddesses of fate. Some of the first groups of deities to be referred to collectively as the fates were a group of judges known as Anunnaki, which were worshipped by the cultures of ancient Mesopotamia.

Leap forward a few thousand years and we find a very famous group of deities who determine the past, the present and the future. These are the Greek Moirai or the Fates. Their names are Clotho, Lachesis and Atropos, and they are daughters of Nyx, the goddess of the night. Interestingly, the Greeks also made one of their sisters, Hemera, the goddess of the dawn. This idea of night (Nyx) giving birth to the light (Hemera) is again echoed in the Norse pantheon with Nott and Jord.

We find another parallel with the Norse and Greek mythologies in the Norns, who again represent the past, present and future. Their names are Urd, Verdandi and Skuld, and it is thought that they visit each newborn child to determine their fate. In some records of the Norse pantheon, these three goddesses become multiple goddesses, one for each human born, but most of the time they are but three.

In the Mari religion, which is a nature-based belief system held by the native people of the republic of Mari El in Russia, the god of fate is Püryshö, and like the Norns from Norse mythology, he determines every individual's future.

In Lithuanian mythology, there are seven goddesses called the Deivės Valdytojos, and they weave the lives of humans into clothes. This is similar to the Fates and the Norns who, as we have seen, are also weavers and spinners of time.

Time frequently pops up in the idioms, phrases and nouns of the English language: borrowed time, time and tide wait for no man, time zones, double time, good times, half time, high time, in the nick of time. I could go on.

In folklore the word 'widdershins' means anticlockwise; however, some believe that this actually links to the sun. In the northern hemisphere, the sun moves clockwise across the sky from east to west. To move against the sun was considered wrong, in fact downright evil, something only engaged in by those who might be witches. Moving against the sun was an anticlockwise movement and therefore, if you did this, you were courting bad luck, plotting evil deeds or conjuring the devil.

Father Time is a personification of the relationship we have with the seconds, minutes and hours of our days. Often appearing in illustrations as an old man with a white beard, a cloak and a stick, he is himself timeless.

There are some superstitions and lore associated with timepieces themselves. Clocks were stopped and fires put out if someone in the house died, so that the departing soul was not distracted.

Back in the field, the sun is here. I have watched it as it slowly makes its way into the sky, only just managing to drag itself above the horizon. For the next sunrise I will be getting up at the same time because of the way we measure time and turn the clocks forward.

I hear the greater woodpecker begin its tattoo upon the trees in the woodland behind me. I make a note to walk back that way to see if I can spot it. Time has stood still whilst I have watched the sunrise, and with no watch or phone to check, my only indication that it is time to head back is the sun above the trees.

When we listen to stories, time moves differently. It slows down as we become immersed in the tale, and within the story itself, time can move differently. This is often so when dealing with the realm of the Celtic fairy, particularly those from Ireland and Wales. Annwn is the name for an other-world that the fae folk inhabit, and if you are not careful, when walking alone at dawn or dusk, you may stray there, pixie-led from the path, taken against your will by one of the other crowd. In general, they will not harm you, but they will very likely entice you to dance until you are exhausted or fall hopelessly in love with one of them. You may find that when they eventually return you to this world, 300 years have passed, when to you it only felt like a day.

I walk back through the woods that are full of scattered light pushing through the branches above. The Japanese call this light Komorebi. This light reminds me of those other-worlds and I feel as if I am walking out of one towards my own. A place where there is structure and time, unlike the field and woods where I have just been.

The story of Oisin (Osheen) tells such a tale of shifting time and it is this tale that I would like to share with you for this month's story. I turn my pockets inside out just in case and head home down the hill.

OISIN AND TÍR NA NÓG

Stories of Oisin (Osheen), the Fianna and Fionn mac Cumhaill (Finn MacCool) are plentiful in Ireland. These stories are collectively known as the Fianna Cycle. They have been told, written down and passed on by many storytellers over the centuries. I have researched this tale by reading several different versions of it and listening to fellow storytellers tell the tales of the warrior-bands known as the Fianna. I hope you will enjoy my interpretation of this ancient Irish tale.

The life of Oisin holds within it many tales of adventure, or echtrai as they are known to the people of Ireland. Oisin is remembered as a warrior of the Fianna, the half-god, half-human son of the great Fionn mac Cumhaill and one of the greatest poets in all of Ireland. This story tells of how Oisin came to be the very last of the mighty Fianna.

Fionn mac Cumhaill was a great hunter. In fact that is how he met Oisin's mother Sadhbh (Sive). Sadhbh had the great misfortune to be cursed for slighting the love of a powerful druid. Fionn had been tracking deer in the forest when he came upon her in doe form and it is said that Fionn broke that curse, and from Sadhbh and Fionn's union, Oisin was born – the little fawn.

However, there was nothing little about Oisin. He was a mighty warrior and legends of his deeds spread far and wide across the land. When he was not defending the Fianna's territories, Oisin too enjoyed the hunt. It was on one of these occasions when he was out hunting with the Fianna that, in an echo of his father's life, he too met his wife to be.

Sitting around the fire sharing noisy stories of their great deeds, the men of the Fianna were hushed as a woman appeared among them. She rode upon a white horse, her golden hair in tresses about her shoulders. Such ethereal beauty did she possess that Oisin immediately fell in love with her.

To the dismay of his comrades, they watched as he fell deeper and deeper in love before their very eyes. The woman introduced herself as Niamh (Neev), daughter of the sea god Manannán mac Lir, and she had travelled far from the land of Tír na nÓg in search of Oisin. She had heard of what a mighty warrior he was and wished for him to be her husband. She told him of how in Tír na nÓg no one grows old, no one wants for anything and peace reigns.

In some stories it is told that Niamh had been cursed with a hog's head and that she asked Oisin to break that curse by marrying her. He therefore could not honourably refuse this request. Perhaps this addition to some of the stories is an attempt to protect Oisin's reputation as a mighty warrior, for how could such a man be taken in by such transparent flattery and overcome with such lust? But Oisin was and the Fianna soon found they were saying goodbye to the son of their leader. Oisin promised to return.

Oisin joined Niamh on her pure white horse and they travelled across the sea until they reached a thick sea fret and through it they rode to the land of eternal youth. Here Oisin became king and ruled with the beautiful Niamh.

Three years passed for Oisin in that land and with it grew a longing. A longing to see his homeland once more and his friends of the Fianna. He asked the permission of Niamh to return, and although she begged him not too, he insisted he must.

Eventually she agreed, handing Oisin the reigns of her white horse to take him home. As Oisin mounted the horse, Niamh looked up at him and begged him to be careful, for all was not as it seemed. She told him he must under no circumstances get down from the horse or he would never return to her in Tír na nÓg.

Oisin set off across the sea and through the mist once more, and soon he was home. Yet it did not look like home; it was much changed. The land was no longer green, forests had disappeared, rivers did not sing so loudly, and when he asked of the warriors of the Fianna he was met with confused faces. When he reached the castle where he once feasted with his father, it lay in ruins and he found no one he recognised.

He drew his horse to a stop in amongst the scattered bricks and broken crenellations. Lost in his grieving for what had happened to the land, Oisin dismounted. As soon as his feet touched the ground, he remembered Niamh's warning, all too late. In fact it had been 300 years since he had left this world, not three. Time caught up with him and his body became frail and aged. Falling to the ground, he could barely speak.

Oisin was found by a priest, who confirmed for him that the Fianna had not walked this land for three centuries. He told him that if he was indeed Oisin, the mighty warrior who had disappeared 300 years ago, then he was in fact the very last of the Fianna.

The priest took Oisin in and nursed him during his last days. With his last breaths Oisin recounted the poetic tales of the Fianna to the priest. It is said that this is how we come to know of them today. It is also said that Oisin and his fairy wife Niamh had children and that they live on in Tír na nÓg. So perhaps there are descendants of the Fianna, and when we have need of such mighty warriors once more, they will hear our call.

TIME DETOX

When we talk about detoxing, we tend to be referring to our diet, which has become sugar, salt and preservative heavy. A detox is a time for us to drink and eat healthily or even to fast, and as a result perhaps to improve our health.

In today's technology-centric world, many also talk of a digital detox. This is characterised by time away from social media, that demanding little red circle on your inbox, or time away from binge-watching YouTube and Netflix. This is often for the benefit of our mental health rather than of our physical bodies.

Arguably, digital and diet detoxes are relatively modern compared to the construct that is time. Look to nature and we can see that it does not require a watch. The sun and the seasons provide ample guidance for their daily, weekly, monthly and annual routines. Our ancestors lived the same way, through the seasons, the sun and the stars.

Of course, these days we have to contend with the rhythms of modern life: work, appointments, events and the twenty-four-hour day. These all happen at a certain time, on a certain date or within certain hours of the day, and we are frequently beholden to them.

For this exercise I'm inviting you to take up the challenge of a time detox – a day without time, or at the very least without watches and other time-measuring devices. If you are feeling ambitious, why not try this for a whole weekend.

There have been several experiments when it comes to living without the construct of time. For example, in the 1960s two scientists, Jürgen Aschoff and Rütger Wever, were keen to see how people coped without a way of telling the time. By placing volunteers in a soundproof bunker with no natural light, it was found that their natural rhythms took over to give them a routine and that these rhythms were reset when they had access to a natural light source once more. The resetting did not take place, as the scientists at first thought, when social influences, such as daily routines, returned.

March or September makes the perfect time of year to try a time detox, as we have near enough equal day and night, giving you a strong anchor for where you are in the day.

Most of us will have lived within the construct of time for the entirety of our lives, so you might find that your routine does not differ particularly, especially as I am suggesting you try this exercise over a relatively short period and that you don't confine yourself to a bunker with no natural light.

You will have the daylight to guide you and perhaps social cues from others, but you may still be surprised by how freeing it feels not to worry about what time it is and simply to eat when you are hungry and sleep when you are tired.

Try to find a day or weekend when you have no commitments, appointments or work. In preparation for your day or weekend, the night before, cover all the clocks and timepieces in your house. Turn your morning alarm off, if you have one set, and place your watch in a cupboard. Don't forget your mobile phone too, as that also has a time on it. So you don't miss anything, you could spend some time the day before noting where you usually look for the time and making sure these places and timepieces are covered or turned off.

You don't have to make any plans for your time detox day(s), but if the idea of having no routine at all fills you with dread then you could simply write yourself out a list of the things you want to do during the day.

During your time detox, try to avoid technology such as the television, computers, smartphones and tablets, as they all have clocks displayed on them somewhere.

Some Ideas for Your Time Detox

Go for a nature walk, find a sit-spot and observe the comings and goings of nature. Don't forget to take a snack and a drink with you.

Read a book from cover to cover.

Keep a journal.

Draw or paint.

Complete your chores without worrying about how long they take you.

Soak in the bath.

Track the journey of the sun across the sky and how it relates to how you are feeling during the day.

Cook a meal from scratch. Cover the time on the cooker and instead watch and smell for when the food is done rather than timing it. One proviso: don't guess if you are cooking meat. Ensure that meat is cooked properly before eating it. Most good cookery books will tell you how to know when meat is cooked, with or without a clock.

For more information and suggestions on time detoxes, take a look at the resources I have put together via the website page that accompanies this book. You will find the web address in the introduction.

APRIL

THE HIRUNDINES RETURN

AS SOON AS I OPEN the door, a tidal wave of sound greets me. This morning has a very different feel to it. With the passing of the equinox, the days now get progressively longer until the longest day in June. The air is full of music and in the canvas of the morning it is as if you can see the crotchets and quavers, dancing across the sky, filling the air.

I can usually pick out different birds amongst the voices, from their unique calls, but my ears and brain are not used to this volume and complexity of song, and it becomes a chaotic symphony of whistles, clicks and trills. Our avian neighbours are putting on a show, staking claim to territories, deciding who will breed this spring and letting the world know they are ready for another season of chick rearing. If you haven't heard the dawn chorus in April, in my humble opinion, you haven't lived.

The dawn chorus is at its peak towards the end of April and through to the beginning of June. It is the order of passerines, more commonly known as songbirds, that sing at this time in the morning and they sing for all the reasons above and for a couple of other reasons too. First, at this time in the morning, the sound carries twenty times as far in the still, calm air. Second, singing comes with a risk and I am not just referring to stage fright. A bird singing loudly advertises its presence to all, friend or foe, but the crepuscular darkness of pre-dawn makes it harder for predators to see them.

Birds such as blackbirds and robins are the first to start singing, as they have the most light-sensitive eyes. In urban environments where there is a lot of light pollution, particularly neon and blue light, this can cause problems for these birds. In some large cities they have been known to sing all night. Exhausting!

So why does the bird that sings the loudest get to secure its place in the gene pool? Well, technically it's the bird that sings the loudest and the longest. Singing uses up energy, so the bird that sings the loudest and longest is clearly the strongest and most likely to father strong chicks. Of course, it's not just the male birds that sing at this time in the morning; the females do too, but they are much quieter.

The crescendo in this joyous ensemble is around half an hour before sunrise, which is exactly the time I stepped out the door this morning, as if called forth by their song.

In 1962, Rachel Carson famously noted the decline in birdsong in the USA. Her book *Silent Spring* led to changes in the law for the use of insecticides, which were not only killing insects but birds as well. However, the decline in bird-song did not stop in the 1960s.

More recently, surveys from across North America and Europe were collected to compare the chorus of birdsong on these continents over the last twenty-five years. The survey shows that there has been a long-standing decline in the variety of bird species singing. This means that with the decline and loss of songbirds, such as the song thrush, night-ingales and skylarks, much of the intricate, layered nature of our soundscapes has also been lost. Researchers have found that the soundscapes of the area where you live are crucial to our sense of belonging. If our soundscapes are being eroded, what does that mean for our sense of belonging?

When I first started this project, I had the idea in my head that I would go to different places to watch the sunrise, but so far I've always returned to the same place, and in this case, familiarity does not breed contempt. It has instead allowed me to connect with my local non-human nature and land-scape on a much deeper level. There is a huge amount of value in understanding a place well, encoding your soul with its rhythms, listening to its soundscape, knowing who your fellow biophilic neighbours are, their toings and froings and where you fit in.

A lack of connection to the land and the nature it holds can ultimately be seen as the key to many of the problems we have today. There is a disconnection with where we came from to the point where we almost forget that we need it. But spend a little time at sunrise in a nearby field, on a bench in your local green space or on the patio of your garden and you'll find it tapping you on the shoulder, reminding you that it's still here; just. All we have to do is reach out, embrace it and keep it safe for the next generation.

My departure from the house to walk the hill to my sit-spot is a little later than usual this morning and as I pass through the village there are some lights on in houses, per-haps because I am a here later or perhaps because people are feeling the effects of spring.

I pass the thrum of the refrigerator fans attached to the local shop; timpani to the bird's woodwind section. The brass section joins in the form of a crow shouting accusingly, 'You're late!' But I still have time to get to my spot on the hill. The sun will not be up for at least another thirty minutes.

I am walking at a brisk pace and I'm warming up quickly. It's a grey, cloud-lined morning that insulates the earth and my winter coat and fleece-lined trousers are not as necessary as they were in February. Behind the clouds on the horizon is a pale passive strip of yellow and an equally fierce strip of orange. The sun is on its way. My unnecessary layers of winter clothes exaggerate the warmth of the morning, which dries my mouth. I can't wait to sit at the top of the hill, drink my coffee and watch the sun make her appearance.

As I reach my sit-spot by the edge of the little copse, looking out across the meadow and the horse jumps, the orange fades and with it comes a lull in the dawn chorus. The pigeons and collared doves calm the other birds with their cooing, and the staccato of great tits and trill of the wren are now easily heard.

I can't feel much of a breeze, but as I sit watching the sky, the cottonwool cumulus clouds tumble across it – a giant crankie show in the sky; I expect shadow puppets to appear at any minute.

Crankies are moving panoramas, scrolls wound from one turning pole to another, often in a miniature theatre-type box or frame. According to the wonderful Bronia Evers, a storyteller specialising in the use of crankies for storytelling, they date from the Victorian era but the first person to call them crankies was Peter Schumann of the Bread and Puppet Theatre established in 1967 in the USA. This term relates to the handles that turn the scroll at either end of the box.

My crankie musings are interrupted by the laugh of the local green woodpecker and the clouds, sandwich-pink streaks of glowing light between them. A new sound joins the cooing and singing; a mewing somewhere between a cat and a baby crying.

I look up and see Mediterranean gulls crossing the meadow south to north. They fly in a follow-my-leader ticker tape across the now lilac sky. In the summer they stop here to collect the insects that fly in plenty above the long grass and it won't be long before they can stop here once more. This morning they are steadfast in their journey and I wonder where they are heading. Perhaps to familiar fields, freshly ploughed and heavy with dew, seeds and earthworms.

Mediterranean gulls are a relatively new addition to our skies. They are local to the northern parts of Europe and the Black Sea. They overwinter in the Mediterranean, but many are now resident on the south coast of England, although the first of these gulls was only spotted in Hampshire in the late 1960s. England now has a current population of around 2,000 birds.

The damp from the grass seeps into my bones, with no promise of a sun bright enough to break through the clouds and warm them. I am glad of the ski trousers now. The sun through the clouds is soft box light and although I can't actually see that the sun is finally up, I know it must be. The rooks have moved in great gaggles from their roosts and this is a sure-fire sign the sun is with us once more.

The stream of seagulls has lasted at least twenty minutes and their occasional mews have been replaced with the territorial squawking of a squirrel vexed by my presence. A little shorter in my sit-spot today, but I shall take the squirrel's cue and head home.

Down the hill and through the village I see the house martins are now awake, feeding their twittering young, clinging to the edge of the mud-cup nests to stuff their hungry mouths with food and then fling themselves back out into the sky to catch more insects.

It's then I see it, high in the clear-blue sky: a twisting, turning, black body with bow-shaped wings. Solitary and silent at first, then there is another, two, three, four and more, all shrieking and darting through the telephone wires and chimney pots. The swifts have returned and it brings joy to my whole being.

These hirundines – house martins, swallows and swifts – are of course following the sun and its analemmatic route across the sky. They seek the place where the earth is tilted most towards the sun, and although it doesn't feel like it today, we are indeed tilting once more. For hirundines to survive, they need the air to be warm and full of the insects that they eat and feed to their burgeoning nests.

They are not the only winged animals to do this. Some migrant butterflies can travel as far as swifts seeking the warmth of the sun. The Painted Lady (*Vanessa cardui*) flies here each summer and has wing sensors that can detect if there is enough sunlight for it to fly. They are tiny solar-panelled beings. The Painted Ladies won't appear until

May, though. Perhaps they are avoiding travelling with the hungry hirundines.

Swifts, swallows and house martins arrive in the UK from far-flung climes between March and June. The first to arrive are the house martins, with a white underside and blue sheen to the black feathers of their head and back. They are the smallest of our three most common hirundines and they are possibly the most familiar to us as their nests are easily spotted beneath the eaves of buildings, but they are actually quite illusive birds.

Currently there is very little information on the migration route of the house martin. They have rarely been seen in the winter in the countries you might expect to find them: South Africa, the west coast of Africa or the Nile Valley. Ornithologists have found ringed house martins on the same routes as the swallows and swifts, but other than that they have yet been able to work out where these birds over-winter.

Swallows are the next to appear in our skies. These birds are easily identified next to their cousins, by the red spot on their throat and their swallowtail. As well as the red spot under their chin they too have a white belly and a blue sheen to the black feathers on their head. Their forked tail has two tail streamers on either side and they can often be seen flying a little lower, above ponds and fields, collecting insects and mud for their nests.

Swifts don't tend to arrive until late April. They have very dark-brown feathers, which can appear black at the beginning of the season but become more bleached in the sun as the season progresses. They are high flyers and their wings and body look like a bow and arrow. Their forked tail is shorter than a swallow's and they are most easily identified by the shrieking sound they make as they are flying. If you've ever heard a swift, it's clear to see how it came by the names 'screecher', 'jack squealer', 'screech martin' and 'shriek owl'. Their Latin name *Apus* means 'without feet', as swifts rarely land and in fact spend the first four years of their life on the wing. Past observers thought this must be because they did not have feet.

More is known about swallow and swift migration, and when they arrive here, they have travelled from the Nile Valley, the west coast of Africa and the Sahara. They fly over Morocco, eastern Spain and the Pyrenees and finally through western France before arriving in the UK. During this 9,000km journey they travel over 300km a day and can fly at speeds of just over 20mph.

It is thought that this need to move on is triggered not just by a drop in temperature, but by the effect that drop has on the density of insects in the air: fewer insects flying around and the birds know it's time to travel south.

There are many hazards facing the hirundines on these epic crossings, starvation being the most obvious, but once they get here, they also face a loss of habitat. Old buildings are being renovated and holes are being filled up in walls and soffits, and these are all places where they like to nest. Swifts pair for life and return to the same sites each year, so if the site has been demolished or 'repaired', they can no longer nest.

As the great naturalist Gilbert White observed in one of his letters, 'Swifts, like sand martins, carry on the business of nidification quite in the dark, in crannies of castles, and towers and steeples and up in the tops of the walls of churches under the roof.' (1877) Isn't 'nidification' a wonderful word for nest building? When I read observations such as this one it often reminds me of stories of towers and castles. Swifts are nature's Rapunzels.

Because of the loss of their homes, swifts are now one of the sixty-plus birds in the UK on the red list of endangered bird species. The best thing you can do for these little wonders is to invest in a swift brick or swift box, and some housing companies are thankfully building these bricks into new houses.

When observing swallows, Gilbert White regularly observed how they collected water from ponds to create mud for their nests. It was also speculated at the time that swallows might even hibernate in ponds beneath the water. Gilbert's thoughts on this were as follows:

> Repeated accounts of this sort, spring and fall, induces us greatly to suspect that house-swallows have some strong attachment to water, independent of the matter of food; and, though they may not retire into that element, yet they may conceal themselves in the banks of pools and rivers during the uncomfortable months of winter. (1877)

Of course, we know now that the swallow disappears because it travels to Africa.

Some of the folklore associated with these feathered beings, in particular the weather lore, was also noted by Gilbert White. He observed that swifts loved thundery weather, perhaps due to an increase in insects in the air. In weather lore, swallows flying low are an indication of rain, whereas if they are high up in the sky, fair weather abounds.

When nesting, swallows only nest in happy, peaceful places and to destroy their nest is very bad luck. This is particularly so in agriculture lore.

Before they return for the winter, swallows will often gather in large flocks and in Norfolk the chattering of these flocks is considered to be the birds gossiping about who will die this winter.

In Chinese culture, the swallow symbolises good fortune and long life. For this reason, some cultures have kept swallows in their homes as living decorations.

As for nicknames, the swallow is sometimes called an 'easin' due its habit of nesting in the eaves and squeezing its way under them in order to do this.

In the world of the sailor, there was a tradition that for every 5,000 nautical miles travelled you would tattoo a swallow on your chest. One on the right and one on the left, both facing in, indicated you were a well-seasoned sailor. These swallows were again considered lucky and they were even thought to carry your soul safely away should you drown at sea.

As you can see from the folklore, it is the swallow that we tell the most stories about. In Aesop's Fables, the swallow represents an animal that has travelled far and therefore is wise and yet roundly ignored by the other animals. The phrase 'one swallow does not a summer make' is also thought to originate from an Aesop's Fable. In this fable it has been a hard winter and a young man has run out of money and cannot feed himself. When he sees a swallow, he thinks the warmer weather has arrived and so he sells his cloak in order to buy food, but he soon discovers his folly when he is frozen to the bone by the last of the winter weather.

I am sharing two stories with you for this chapter, both of which are fables explaining how the swallow got its forked tail.

THE LEGEND OF ERKHII MERGEN

This story originates from Mongolia and I have found different versions from a variety of different sources, both online and in books. This is my interpretation of this ancient tale of the sun and swallows.

There was once a time when the earth had seven suns. These were not easy times. The world was hot, food and water were scarce, and everyone saw the world through squinting eyes.

During this time there lived a magnificent archer called Erkhii Mergen. He had dedicated his life to the art and was now a mighty warrior. With the riverbeds dry, the fields bare and the animals and people dying, Erkhii understood his calling. The people needed him – they needed his skill and it was up to him to end the tyranny of the suns.

So Erkhii took up his bow and arrow, saddled his horse and rode across the land until he was standing on the horizon where he faced the seven suns. He drew back his bow and fired an arrow into the first sun. It found its mark and the sun disappeared over the horizon. Then he fired a second at the second sun, a third, a fourth and so on, until there was one sun and one arrow left.

Swallow had been watching and Swallow knew that no suns was as bad as seven suns, and when Erkhii drew back his bow and let the seventh arrow fly, Swallow also flew true and intercepted the arrow. This arrow split Swallow's tail in two and fell to the ground, just short of the seventh sun.

It is said that Erkhii was so frustrated and ashamed that he had not achieve his task that he cut off his own thumbs so that he might never hold a bow again.

To this day we have one sun, the swallow has a forked tail and Erkhii Mergen roams the wilderness as the thumbless rodent that is known as a marmot.

THE SWALLOW AND THE SNAKE

I found this next story in a book of nature myths by Florence Holbrook published in 1902 in Chicago. In the introduction, reference is made to this collection of stories coming from folklore and potentially the oral storytelling traditions. It appears in various forms across the internet.

Each day the animals of the world would gather around the feet of the Great Creator to seek an audience, with the hope that they could have their grievances heard. Every day the Great Creator did their best to solve the problems of the world.

On this particular day it was Human's turn to speak.

'My complaint, Great Creator, is that Snake delights in the taste of my blood. I do not think this should be so.'

'Come forward, Snake,' said the Creator and Snake slithered forward. 'Is this true?'

'It is,' replied Snake. 'Human's blood is by far the tastiest.'

Swallow did not like what it heard. Human was a friend to Swallow. Human allowed it to nest in the eaves of houses and delighted in its song, so Swallow was pleased when the Great Creator sent Mosquito, the connoisseur of blood, out into the world to discover which creature's blood tasted the best. Swallow felt sure Mosquito would come back with an alternative, but Swallow needed to make sure.

Swallow waited for Mosquito to return and intercepted Mosquito as it did.

'So, tell me, which animal has the tastiest blood?' asked Swallow.

'Human, of course,' replied Mosquito. 'There is no denying it. Snake is correct and I am off to tell the Great Creator now!'

'Hang on,' said Swallow. 'Before you do, let me see the tongue that has tasted this delicious blood.'

Mosquito obliged, sticking his tongue out for Swallow to inspect. Quick as a flash Swallow bit off Mosquito's tongue and when Mosquito appeared before the Great Creator it could not speak.

'I will speak for Mosquito,' said Swallow. 'Mosquito must be a little timid in your presence, oh great one, or perhaps tired from the journey, but Mosquito spoke to me on its return.'

'Very well, Swallow, and what did Mosquito say?'

'Mosquito tasted the blood of all the creatures and declared Frog's to be the best,' announced Swallow.

Mosquito was incensed but the only noise it could make was a buzzing sound and the Great Creator took this to be agreement.

'Very well,' said the Great Creator. 'From now on Frog will be the food of Snake.'

Snake did not like frogs at all. Their slimy flesh tasted like pondweed. Snake blamed Swallow for this outcome and launched itself at the bird, which flew up into the air and away, but not quickly enough, for Snake managed to take a bite out of Swallow's tail, and that is why, to this day, like the forked tongue of the snake, Swallow has a forked tail.

SUNRISE SOUNDSCAPE

I love soundscapes and I often use them in my work in heritage interpretation. They are extremely evocative and, as mentioned earlier in this chapter, they are of vital importance when it comes to our sense of belonging.

For this exercise I am inviting you to record your local soundscape. It doesn't have to be early in the morning, but you may find it easier at this time. All you will need is yourself and something to record your soundscape. Most mobile devices allow you to do this these days or there are apps you can download.

I would highly recommend getting out early at this time of year to listen to the dawn chorus, which in the UK is around 6–6.30 a.m. It's also a chance to soak up some of the vitamin D we have so missed in the winter.

Ideas for Soundscapes

Your usual walk, or perhaps a dog walk or a daily run
Your kitchen whilst cooking dinner
Your back garden or doorstep
A spot in your local green space or wood where you can sit for a while and make your recording
The sounds of your favourite holiday spot
The local allotment
A trip to your local nature reserve
A walk along the beach

You can find an example of a soundscape I created on the website page that accompanies this book. You will find the web address in the introduction.

MAY

FIRE STORY

BLACKBIRDS ARE A REGULAR COMPANION on these sunrise vigils, and as I walk along the pavement in the village, they are not just on every set of ridge tiles, but on the guttering, chimney pots and dormer windows of countless houses. This glossy black player of the golden flute is not at all shy at this time in the morning and its song is shrill, demanding and proud. In Ireland, if the song of a blackbird is particularly loud, it is thought to herald rain, but the dark grey patches on the footpath tell me this has already been and gone.

In northern Italy, in the town of Brescia, the last few days of January are known as *I giorni della merla* or 'the days of the blackbird'. The story goes that the blackbird was once white, but the last days in January were so cold that it had to hide in a chimney and from this retained its black feathers forever more.

This morning it is a reasonably mild 10°C compared to the bold, cold and bitter winds of January. There is a bright quarter moon in the sky and glittering slugs litter the footpaths, soaking up last night's rain. My eyes are focusing on the pavement as I try to avoid committing slugicide, when I hear a voice ring out above the blackbirds. I pause, and look up. It's not one voice but two. Two song thrushes, one on either end of a row of brick-red ridge tiles. This bird was, until very recently, red-listed but in December 2021 it moved to amber status. It's still in need of our help but thankfully has been brought back from the edge of extinction.

I am privileged to be very familiar with its song as the resident song thrush sits in my neighbour's tree and sings from about four in the morning during the summer months. I am pleased to see it doing so well, even if four in the morning isn't ideal for my required sleep quota.

The song thrush, in some parts of the UK, is nicknamed the 'storm cock' for its habit of singing from the tops of trees into the prevailing wind of an incoming storm. In Germany, the blackbird is sometimes called *Gottling*, meaning 'little god', as, if one is kept in the house, it offers protection from lightning strike.

With these birds side by side, at least if there is a storm, I will be safe. But the sky is a clear soft cobalt blue and tiny stars still hang in it with not a hint of cumulonimbus to warn of a storm. The twilight lasts much longer now, and although I can still see clearly, there is an otherworldliness to the light.

The horse chestnut tree is piled high with tiered, luminescent blooms, which would not be out of place next to the pyramids of profiteroles and macarons found in Parisian patisseries.

I cross the road and start to walk up the footpath to the meadow. In the half-light, I trip clumsily on lumps of downland chalk, sending them clattering along the path. Rows of heads appear above the grass. White-tailed bunnies enjoying their breakfast view me warily. With all the bows of green foliage that corridor the path I cannot see across the hill, as I have been able to before; instead it makes a tunnel, under which I walk, blind to what lays either side of the hedge.

I hear something large moving ahead. My senses tell me to look to my left, and around the corner, as the trees break, I see a doe and her fawn not more than 5m away, staring at me, as surprised as I am. I stand still and watch them watching me, watching them. Her face is enquiring. What am I doing here at this time in the morning? But as soon as I step forward to explain, she barks and is off into the gloaming. I wonder if her fawn is the progeny of the roe buck whose field I sit in?

I reach the meadow and the grass is knee high. The dew condenses and drifts upwards as the ground slowly warms and a haze hangs above the meadow. A path has been mown through the grass to allow walkers across it without disturbing the wildflowers and insects, and it is pitted with jewelled sheet webs. My old friend the tawny owl is still calling as I find my sit-spot and settle in for the show.

The view this morning is akin to a Pre-Raphaelite painting with streaks of blue, pink and lilac daubed across the sky.

Every blade of grass has a drop of dew on it and the seeping light illuminates each tiny orb.

The Mediterranean gulls, which in March flew straight over the field, now stop to gather insects in the long grass. The church bells tell me it's five o'clock. Mani is to my right and Sol is about to appear on my left.

I am sitting a little bit further down the hill today to avoid trampling any wildflowers, and the height of the grass, in front of me and behind me, means I am cocooned in the landscape.

The sun begins to rise; an orange fiery disc that drags the mist up from the grass, with it. As it creeps up over the trees, I feel the warmth on my face, thawing my cold, damp bones. The whitewashed houses down in the valley become beacons, and vapour trails in the sky fluoresce. A sound rises up inside me and I find that I am humming, singing to the earth as I feel the same emotive force that motivated our ancestors to celebrate this wondrous star with song and dance.

For thousands of years there have been festivals across Europe celebrating the passing of April into May and the growing warmth of the sun, the produce it brings and its power. These festivals have gone by many different names but ironically never Beltane or Beltain. This is because Beltane was actually defined as a ritual rather than a festival. The research of Professor Ronald Hutton, a well-respected expert on the history, traditions and customs of the British Isles, has shown that Beltane was actually referring to a way of blessing the cattle and those who were going to drive the livestock up to the fields for the summer grazing. The ritual would have involved walking cattle between two enormous balefires in order to bring them good fortune for the coming year. It is thought the smoke from the fires would also have rid the cattle of any flies or tics they had.

It is widely believed the bale in balefire relates to 'bel' in Beltane, which also means fire. This then brings us to Bel, also known as Belinus, Belli and Bile, a Celtic sun god with ancient roots. For the Celts, each year on 30 April or 1 May the union of Belinus the sun god and Danu or Don the earth goddess is celebrated. In the wheel of the year this is called a cross-quarter festival, as it falls between the vernal equinox in March and the summer solstice in June, and it celebrates life and the abundance that will soon come with the summer. The marriage of Belinus and Danu is also representative of the union between heaven and earth or, in nature's terms, the sky and the earth.

Belinus' roots can be traced back to the Phoenician god Baal, which means 'bright' in Gaelic. The goddess Danu is older still – she dates back to 10,000 BCE. Her name is sometimes translated as 'river' and from her comes all life.

Danu is the mother of all the Irish gods and goddesses. She and Belinus unite and produce two acorns, which fall into the river, and from these acorns come Brigid and Dagda, who in turn created the Children of the Danu, also known as the Tuatha Dé Danann, the first inhabitants of Ireland.

Beltane could therefore be seen as a re-enactment of this union and subsequent birth of a nation with fires, which are lit across the country. In Ireland the festival was not called Beltane, though. It was called Cétamain. Traditions include couples jumping the fire to bring them fertility and to bless their home.

In Wales there is a similar tradition of lighting fires on what is called Calan Mai or Calan Haf, meaning the first day of May or summer. Bonfires are lit using what is referred to as 'wild fire'. This fire is created using a spark stick, which consists of one horizontal stick with a hole in it and a second vertical stick inserted into the hole and turned to create friction until a spark is created. This also occurred in the Highlands of Scotland in the eighteenth century. The ritual involved nine men taking nine shifts in order to get the stick to spark. The fires were again used to bless cattle.

There are many other examples across Europe of fires being used at this time of year to celebrate the coming of spring and mark long-standing fertility rituals and festivals.

Today across the UK, there are many villages, heritage sites and places of spiritual importance that hold Beltane festivals. Butser Ancient Farm, in the South Downs, is one of these and I am lucky enough to live very close to this heritage site and centre for experimental archaeology.

I am a regular storyteller in the Butser roundhouses and I am a member of Herigeas Hundas, a wonderful group of re-enactors who also call the farm their home. As you might expect, when I am with Herigeas Hundas, I am their Scop/Storyteller, named Furspel, meaning 'fire-story', and alongside our cunning woman, lyre player, blacksmiths, warriors and archers, I attend Beltane at Butser Ancient Farm. The tagline for this event is 'Stand in the Glow', as at end of the evening a giant 12m-tall wicker man of varying design is set alight to celebrate the fire festival. This is the farm's biggest event of the year and around 3,000 people attend to watch morris dancing, live music and re-enactments, peruse stallholders' wares and, of course, to eat, drink and be merry.

The wonderful Hampshire Astronomical group, known as Hants Astro, also attend this festival, bringing, in addition to their telescopes for stargazing later in the evening, solar 'finderscopes' that allow you to view the sun without damaging your eyes.

I can't resist and as I look through the scope all I can see is an orb of bright yellow light that fills my view. For a moment I can't see that it is actually the sun. It takes me a while to realise that it is so huge, it is filling the whole viewfinder!

They have different telescopes set up to view different elements of the sun. The guide lets me know that I'm looking for solar flares through this scope. Once I've got my eye in, I see tiny tufts at the very top of the deep yellow disc, like the cow licks of hair on Charlie Brown in the Peanut cartoons. These are the solar flares and I'm told that these flares are actually fifteen times the height of the earth.

In the next scope I'm shown sunspots, tiny, dark pinpricks on the surface of the sun, which are actually ten times the size of earth. I am in awe. It is awesome.

The tiny spots of black that I am looking at on the surface of the sun are places on the sun that are cooler than the rest of it, but that's only relatively so – they are still in excess of 6,000°F.

These spots on the sun often precede a solar flare, one of those cartoon hair tufts. Solar flares are abrupt and intense discharges of energy from the sun, and this solar activity activates gases in our magnetosphere, which in turn creates the beautiful green and blue, undulating auroras that can be seen nearer the poles.

To gaze upon the surface of the sun is a privilege indeed and one I don't suggest you experience without the proper equipment. However, if you get the opportunity, the sun's power is undeniable – though we haven't always been allowed to acknowledge it.

Over 400 years ago the great philosopher, astronomer and mathematician, Galileo, landed himself in a lot of trouble with the Catholic Church when he wrote a series of letters about sunspots. At the forefront of science and discovery, Galileo theorised, quite correctly, that the sun was the centre of our solar system and that the earth travelled around it. This is called a heliocentric model, whereas the Catholic Church believed in an earth-centric model. Suggesting that his heliocentric model was scientific fact led to Galileo being branded a heretic by the Catholic Church.

Galileo published further findings in 1610 in a book called *The Starry Messenger* and continued to research his theories until, in 1633, the Catholic Church could tolerate it no longer and, at the age of 70, Galileo was placed under house arrest. There he remained for the rest of his life, incarcerated by man's obstinacy when it came to the sun.

At Beltane, as the evening comes to a close, the wicker man must meet his fate. Amongst the crowds gathered to celebrate, I hear the drums as they vibrate the earth, the bells of the morris dancers ringing out, the crowd's whoops and cheers, and then he is alight! Back in the meadow where I sit for my May sunrise, the sun too is alight, high in the sky.

I make my way back along the mown path towards the woods, where I will follow the path down the hill and into the village. On the other side of the long grass, there are nettles and brambles edging the woodland and here, this morning, I encounter masses of snails. Rounded snails, copse snails, brown-lipped, white-lipped, banded and Pomatiidae. A Dulux colour chart of browns, swirls of yellow and tortoiseshell spirals.

It was once thought that snails died and were reborn, as they disappeared into their shells during the sun's heat and reappeared as the damp crept into the earth once more. At Lambeth Palace in London there is a stained-glass window called the Resurrection Window, created to celebrate the resurrection of Christ in the Christian religion. If you look at the window, you will find three snails representing rebirth

This symbolism goes much further back to Aztec culture when the snail was also considered to represent the cycle of life. In Greek mythology it is said that Nerites, son of the sea god Nereus, challenged Helios, the god of the sun, to a chariot race. When he did not win, he was transformed into a sea snail; another conflict between the sun and a snail. This morning, it is the rain that has reanimated the snails.

With the rain comes fresh new growth and there is an iridescent glow to the chartreuse green of the trees. The wood looks different, feels different, and smells different. Desire paths, created by small animals, are clear in the undergrowth, inviting you to walk along them, and the pigeons' clapping alarm calls are softened by the foliage.

The great greening is here and now the blossoming has begun in the hedgerows and the woodland canopies: hawthorn, horse chestnut, elm, wild cherry and elderflower. I am reminded once more of the flower goddesses of old and their inextricable link with the fertility of the sun.

The Romans celebrated the festival of Floralia, in which the goddess Flora was invoked to bless the spring blossoms and bring abundance in the summer. During this festival a flurry of flowers bedecked temples, people and the streets. Over 2,000 years later in the town of Helston in the UK, echoes of this festival can be found in Flora Day, celebrated ever year with dancing, music and, of course, copious flowers.

In 2021 the National Trust launched an initiative called Blossom Watch, in which people are encouraged to share pictures of the wonderful tree blossoms that are bursting into life at this time of year and to remember the importance of flowering plants as more than just aesthetics. They are a vital life source fuelled by the union of the sun and the earth.

The flower goddess motif also appears in Welsh mythology as Blodeuwedd (bluh-dye-eth). She is one of the main characters in the fourth branch of the Mabinogion. The Mabinogion is a text originating from the twelfth century, one of the oldest texts of its kind, which comprises a collection of stories from Welsh mythology.

The story goes that Blodeuwedd is brought into being to provide a wife for Lleu Llaw Gyffs. His mother Arianrhod, who is a sun goddess, has cursed Lleu so that he cannot marry a human and Blodeuwedd is made for him out of oak, broom and meadowsweet. In Ireland, Lleu Llaw Gyffs is known as Lugh, again a sun god, and so the union of Blodeuwedd and Lleu in the Mabinogion is reminiscent of the marriage between Belinus the sun god and Danu the earth goddess. Blodeuwedd is the land and Lleu is the sun.

It could also be said that, like the flowers, she represents the female aspect of nature, created purely for the benefit of procreation and to secure Lleu's rule in his kingdom. However, Blodeuwedd does not settle for her lot in life, and so her fate is also inextricably linked with that liminal space between night and day, and for me the untamed power that resides within her is like that of the sun within the blossoms of the trees.

BLODEUWEDD THE FLOWER GODDESS

This story comes from the fourth branch of the Mabinogion, entitled Map ap Mathonwy. The branches in this text are named after the lead male characters, in this case Math, but for me Blodeuwedd is the star of this show. There are many versions and translations of the Mabinogion. It has been told many times by storytellers over hundreds of years. This is my interpretation of Blodeuwedd's story.

When the folk of magic walked among us there was one named Math who could not. King of Gwynedd, he could not exist in our world unless his feet were resting in the lap of a woman, and this foot-holder, whether she was deity, fae folk or mortal, could not have carnal knowledge of another.

And even though Math could go where he wished in his world, he could not move and walk among us unless he was at war, and so it was that his nephews, Gwydion and Gilfaethwy, sons of earth goddess Don, went out in his place. They travelled to and from the great cities conducting Math's business for him, but they were not always allies of Math.

At that time, Math had a particularly charming foot-holder named Goewin and it soon became apparent to Gwydion that his cousin Gilfaethwy was in love with her. He could hide it from Math but not from his cousin. Gwydion was a silver-tongued trickster and magician, and he spoke to his cousin of a plan he had to win Goewin for him. Gilfaethwy, consumed with lust for the foot-holder, agreed to conduct the plan with Gwydion. Knowing that Math could only walk on the earth if he was at war, they devised to set the kingdom of Gwynedd at war with the kingdom of Dyfed.

First, they spoke to their uncle and told him of the won-drous and magical pigs owned by the King of Dyfed. Math naturally wished to possess these pigs as proof of his great power, and so he sent Gilfaethwy and Gwydion to retrieve them. Gwydion disguised himself and tricked Pryderi, King of Dyfed, to part with the pigs in exchange for a number of pedigree horses and dogs.

Gwydion returned to Gwynedd with the pigs and Math was most pleased with the gift. However, in Dyfed, Pryderi soon realised the dogs and horses were an illusion, magicked up by the trickster Gwydion, and set off to wage war on Gwynedd. And so it was that Math rode out to meet Pryderi on the battlefield, leaving his foot-holder Goewin alone and at the mercy of his nephews.

While Math was away, Gilfaethwy forced himself on Goewin. When Math returned, Goewin was distraught and

Math was furious with his nephews. He punished them by turning them into first deer, then boars and then wolves, leaving them to roam the forests as each animal for a year, so that they might know the fear of being hunted.

When the nephews were at last free of their triptych of punishment, Gwydion offered up his sister Arianrhod as Math's next foot-holder. Arianrhod was the goddess of the dawn and also the daughter of Don. Math was enthused by this idea, but he did not trust his nephew. He had good reason not to.

He called Arianrhod to him and tested her chastity by asking her to step over a branch of the rowan tree. From her fell not one child but two. The first was picked up by Math, baptised in the sea and named Dylan. Gwydion concealed the second before anyone could see him, for Gwydion knew that these children were his. He had come to his sister in the night disguised as another and laid with her whilst she was sleeping. She had no knowledge of this and now she was standing in front of the court of Math unable to defend herself.

Years passed and Arianrhod could not shake off her shame or ignore the judgement in the eyes of others, and so the shame turned to anger and bitter hatred. When she discovered that all this time her brother Gwydion had kept the second child and brought him up as his own, and that in fact the child was her brother's, then the fire within her became solar; untamed and wild.

She cursed the child and said that he would never have a name unless it was one that she gave him, and she would never do that. This would not do, for someone that had the favour of Math and would one day rule in his place could not do so without a name.

Of course, Gwydion found a way around this, disguising himself and the boy as purveyors of the finest leather shoes in all the colours found in the Black Mountains.

Arianrhod had never seen anything like them before. She complemented the traders she saw before her and called the boy fair and skilful. Gwydion then revealed himself and told Arianrhod that she had given her son a name, and that name was Lleu Llaw Gyffes, meaning 'fair one with a skilful hand'.

Arianrhod's anger rose once more and she cursed the boy, foretelling that he would never hold a weapon unless she placed that weapon in his hand. Again, this would not do, for how was Lleu to defend his kingdom without holding a weapon?

When the kingdom was at war once more, Gwydion disguised himself and Lleu Llaw Gyffes as bards, begging an audience with Arianrhod to offer themselves up as soldiers for the cause. And so, it came about that she handed her son a sword and a shield, and her curse was broken again.

This time Arianrhod thought carefully about her curse and the third was by far the worst, for in this court of men it jeopardised Lleu's ability to continue his line. He would have no human wife.

Gwydion went to Math to seek help. Math then went with Gwydion and Lleu into the woods to work magic and conjure his great-nephew a wife. They created her from oak, broom and meadowsweet. This ivory and yellow flower-faced goddess was named Blodeuedd, and she and Lleu Llaw Gyffes married, securing his place within the royal family.

Blodeuedd was a beautiful being, born out of men and magic, but her soul was hers and hers alone. She had arrived in this world as an adult; she had had no time to grow into her role. She was bored with the fighting and hunting that continued in cycle after cycle, and she did not love her husband. She did not understand the rules of the land – how, once you were married, you could not be with any other man; that your reason for being was your husband. Of course, her creation was the very personification of this, but within her Blodeuedd still knew the wild and untamed forest. It was in every one of her delicate blooms. It ran through the stems of each flower and lived in the pollen of her stamen. She was a child of the forest.

She spent many of her days in the court, confused and without purpose, until one day there arrived a man: Gronw Pebyr, a member of a visiting lord's hunting party. It was then that all the pieces of her life fell into place. She had been created for Lleu Llaw Gyffes, yes, but she was not meant for him. She was meant for Gronw and she could feel it in every part of her being.

The meadowsweet, broom and oak bloomed brighter in his presence and he saw that. But she was the wife of Lleu Llaw Gyffes, nephew of Math, heir to the throne of Gwynedd. Not only that, but Math had blessed Lleu Llaw Gyffes so that he might not be killed in any of the usual ways. He could only die naturally or in a very particular set of circumstances, so how was Blodeuedd to set herself free?

Blodeuedd brooded on her problem and Lleu saw that his wife did not have her usual practised smile upon her face. He asked her what was wrong and she at last saw how she could reclaim her autonomy.

She replied that she was worried that he would be killed and taken from her. He answered that he could not be killed, for he had the blood and the blessing of the ever-living ones in his very veins. As the great-nephew of Math, this could not be undone.

'But I do so worry', she replied.

'You should not. There is only one way that I can be killed and the circumstances that allow this are so unlikely to occur that there really is nothing to worry about,' her husband reassured her.

'Lleu, tell me what they are, so that I may protect you from them,' she replied.

Lleu laughed and in his assured arrogance told her, 'I cannot be killed on horseback nor foot, nor indoors nor outdoors.'

'But how can this be?' she replied, and Lleu took her crest-fallen face for a sign of distress.

'It is very simple. I must run myself a bath that is beside the river. This bath must be beneath a thatched roof and I must place one foot on the bath and one on the back of a wild goat. When all this is done, I can still only be killed by a spear that has been a year in the crafting.'

'I'll rest a little easier now, husband, although I insist that you take care, for there are many things that I have not seen in this world, but I know from what little experience I have that this does not mean they do not exist or cannot come into being.'

Lleu laughed once more and was soon away to battle again at the side of his uncle.

Blodeuedd went to Gronw and told him of what she had discovered. He thought it impossible, but she told him that if he could craft the spear, she would do the rest.

A year later, Lleu returned to find Blodeuedd sorrowful once more. She told him that she had been so concerned about him during his absence that he must set her mind at ease. He must show her exactly how impossible it was to kill him.

Lleu, who had survived battle after battle, wound after wound, whilst all about him were slain, agreed to do this. He instructed Blodeuedd to source the bath, the thatched canopy and the goat, and he would show her how, even with all these things, he could not be killed.

She did this, but she also fetched Gronw with his spear and instructed him to hide until she gave the signal.

Beside the river, Lleu filled the bath and stood beneath the thatched canopy with one foot on the goat and one on the bath.

'You see,' he said. 'Impossible! For even if all of this is constructed for me, there is still no one with the spear that can kill me.'

It was at this moment that Gronw rose from his hiding place and thrust the spear into the air in a soaring arc, where it eventually met its mark in Lleu's chest.

Thinking him dead, the lovers ran whilst high above them a dying Lleu in the shape of an eagle flew away to find cover.

With Gronw and Blodeuedd missing and Lleu nowhere to be found, the search began. Of course, Math and Gwydion found Lleu before all life had left him, and with more magic restored his immortality. Lleu hunted down Blodeuedd and her lover. He killed Gronw and turned Blodeuedd into Blodeuwedd. She was no longer flower-faced but owl-faced, and one who would never again look upon the sun. The wife of a god born of a sun goddess, a woman who was herself created from the flowers that harnessed the power of the sun, she was now destined to inhabit the night.

A CELEBRATION OF LIGHT

What better way is there to celebrate the sun and the deities of light than with fire? Many gardens have chimeneas, table-top fire pits and lanterns, and these are all delightfully cosy ways to hold onto the light in your garden, after the sun goes down. But we might not have these things available to us or an outdoor space to enjoy them in, so here's a really simple ritual to bring the power of the sun into your home.

You Will Need

A terracotta plant-pot saucer, 20cm in diameter
One pillar candle, 8–10cm in diameter or smaller if you wish
Stones, pebbles or glass discs – the kind used in floristry to fill glass vases
Flowers and blossoms from your garden, or a bunch of seasonal flowers

How to Prepare

Place the candle in the middle of the terracotta saucer. If you want to use a smaller candle and saucer then you can. Place stones, pebbles and/or the glass discs around the bottom of the candle. Build them up around the base of the candle, as this will help steady it. Scatter petals and flower heads from seasonal flowers on top of the stones in the saucer.

You can use whatever colour candle you like, but colours that are associated with the sun deities are red, yellow, gold, orange, white and silver. You might also consider using a citronella candle if you are outside in the garden, as citronella is great for keeping at bay the rampant, nibbling midges present at this time of year.

Find a suitable place for your candle and saucer that is safe and away from anything that might catch alight. The dining room table is often a good place. If you are lucky enough to have a fireplace, you could place it in the hearth. Otherwise, you could place it on a flat surface in the garden.

As you light the candle, you could offer a little incantation for the sun to harness its power and prosperity for the coming summer. Here's an example.

An Incantation for the Sun

Belios and Danu I call on you
Bless this place with love,
Fill this place with joy
Bring this place prosperity
As the sun strengthens its light
So mote it be.

JUNE

STANDSTILL

I NEED TO TAKE YOU back to March for the beginning of this chapter and the A303 trunk road that will take you from Basingstoke in Hampshire to Honiton in Devon, crossing five counties.

It's almost 7 a.m. and a friend and I are on our way to commune with some very famous stones. As we cross the border from Hampshire to Wiltshire, the sun is still red on the horizon. On the way across the edge of the South Downs, out of the driver-side window, Sue spots enormous hares bounding across the countryside. The downland now behind us, we are travelling a road that has in one form or another been a part of our landscape for thousands of years.

The A303, for many, is a holiday route to the West Country. Tom Fort calls it a 'highway to the sun' in his book of the same title. I too have memories of travelling to Devon to stay with my grandmother in the little fishing village of Appledore. I remember sunny days rock pooling, sitting on the harbour wall crabbing, eating clotted cream ice cream, and even a trip to take a look around an RNLI lifeboat, on which the decks were made of black rubber and it was so hot that it was impossible to stand on them with our bare feet. But today, whilst Sue and I are in search of the sun, our aim is to connect with the landscape in a very different way, not through sandcastles and ice cream but through megaliths and barrows.

We are on our way to Stonehenge for what English Heritage bills as a 'Stone Circle Experience'; a chance to stand amongst the ancient megaliths, famous for their connection with the sun.

To give you some background on access rights to Stonehenge and why you now need to buy a ticket or apply via managed open access, we need to go back to 1977 when the stones were first roped off.

This decision was made by the Department of Environment and was an effort to preserve the stones, to prevent soil erosion around them and wear and tear to the stones themselves. In 1984 English Heritage took over the preservation of Stonehenge and at this point there were still a large number of people visiting the stones for the solstice. The encampments during this time had been going on for many, many years and people camped around the stones to celebrate the sun. The new custodians of the stones discovered that these encampments, as they grew in size, were at risk of damaging the stones and the archaeology that undoubtedly lay beneath the tent pitches.

In June 1985, English Heritage applied for an injunction to stop these encampments and was given it. This resulted in the famous 'Battle of the Beanfield'; a dark day in the history of Stonehenge. I will not linger too long on these events, but they are important in the history of our land. If you are not aware of this historic event, I urge you to find out about it. It was not until another fifteen years had passed and the millennium arrived in 2000 that those celebrating the solstice as part of their spiritual practice were given access to the stones once more.

Since then, visitors have been able to walk amongst the stones via early morning Stonehenge Experiences or on very special occasions such as the summer and winter solstice festivals and both the equinoxes. During the festivals, access to the stones is free under English Heritage's managed open access agreement, and those visiting are asked to stick to guidelines that help to preserve the stones and to keep everyone safe. There can be as many as 7,000 people gathered for the summer solstice.

The summer solstice is defined as the longest day and the shortest night of the year and the word itself comes from the two Latin words *sol* and *sistere*, which combine to mean 'sun stand still'. For three days around 21–23 of June, to our ancestors and indeed to us if we are paying attention, the sun looks like it is at a standstill in the sky.

Up until this point it has appeared to get gradually higher and higher. At this point in its journey, the northern hemisphere is tilted towards the sun and therefore the solstice marks the moment when the earth's northern hemisphere reaches its closest point to the sun and therefore the point where we have the longest days. Because of the tilt, the southern hemisphere is pointed away from the sun, so summer solstice does not occur in the southern hemisphere until December when the earth has tilted back towards the sun again.

At this time of year, the earth is positioned in such a way that those living in the farthest north on our planet will experience twenty-four hours of sunlight each day.

Standing stones such as Stonehenge are thought to create a link between the earth and the sky, and for thousands of years it seems that they have been used for rituals marking and celebrating solar events. They predate the pyramids.

Archeoastronomers, specialists who study our ancestors' link to the stars, have been able to work out how old various standing stones are, based on where the sun is now and where it was likely to have been at the time the stones were erected. For example, if a standing stone is two solar widths to the left of the sun as it appears in the sky now, that dates the megalith as 5,000 years old. Stonehenge is thought to be of a similar age, although it's not as easy to work this out as the stones have been laid down and stood up again at various points in history.

At no point in my lifetime have the megaliths at Stonehenge been open access and yet they are very familiar to me. Perhaps it is that ancestral *Qi* I spoke about in the introduction. Stepping into the circle of 4m-tall sarsen stones, the sun on your face and the wind in your hair, these monuments sing to your soul with a very visceral note. On this March morning, squinting in the light as the sun appears and disappears through the circle of stones like a zoetrope, they tower above me and even those that have fallen cannot fail to impress me with their might.

Huddled inside these sarsens are the smaller Preseli blue stones. These stones weigh between 2 and 5 tons each with the largest sarsen stone weighing 25 tonnes.

Outside stands the heel stone, weighing in at 35 tonnes, which patiently waits to mark the path of the sun on the summer and winter solstices. Between the heel stone and the sarsen stones of the circle lies the fallen Slaughter stone. It was given its rather gruesome name by the Victorians, who never missed a chance for drama and were inspired by the iron ore within the stone that tinged it red and made it look as if blood had been spilled upon it.

The stones must have travelled at least 25 kilometres to reach this destination and it is estimated that it would have taken around 1,000 people to complete the task.

A ditch surrounds the circle, which is what makes it a henge. Sue beckons to me from the ditch. She has discovered that if you take a moment to stand in the ditch, the stones become a part of the landscape, sunken into it, and all the people around the bottom of it disappear. All there is, is you, the earth and the singing skylarks. I discover this as I join her in the ditch. Sometimes it pays to hang around in ditches.

Despite the clearance of many of the trees that would have stood here, there is much life in this landscape. As the stones soak up the light of the sun, they have become home to over seventy different lichens, some extremely rare. There is even a type of marine lichen here that has somehow found a way to grow.

The crows and jackdaws gather here and hares hide out in the stones at night. The hares are well used to the staff who look after the stones, and I am told by the guide, Wendy, that the security guards who patrol the stones twenty-four/seven often shine their lights on the hare scrapes, and if the hares are not there, they know someone who shouldn't be is in amongst the stones. A rather excellent way of telling, I think.

There are many human marks on the stones from the years before 1977. The shape of a sword, a Bronze Age axe, names carved into the stones and shells from the two world wars embedded there almost a century ago, all have become a physical record of the history these stones have seen.

For a long time, visitors to Stonehenge were able to take pieces of the stones and there are marks that show where people chipped away at them for their souvenir – in some cases, dangerously so, resulting in concrete having to be inserted into the bottom of one stone in order to stop it falling.

It is thought this practice had gone on for centuries, as in the eleventh century, Geoffrey of Monmouth, a popular chronicler of the time, noted that many believed the Preseli blue stone had healing properties. Of course, this is neither safe nor in the spirit of preserving heritage for the next generation, and the practice is no longer allowed.

Stonehenge may be one of the most famous megaliths in the world, particularly because of its significance and continued status as a place of celebration during the solstices, but it is not the only standing stone thought to have been used for this purpose.

If you had the opportunity to visit the World of Stonehenge Exhibition in London in 2022, you will have discovered that these stones can be found all over Europe and come in many shapes and sizes. Often, they feature scenes that include the sun, farming life and gatherings, or spiral symbols carved onto the stone. It is thought that the universal patterns found on many of the stones in Britain and Ireland, such as spirals, were a way of creating connections and a language through art that could be read by all. This art recorded the seasons and the rituals associated with the turning of the wheel, and in many cases the stones themselves are positioned in alignment with the sun at particular times of year.

Timber henges are also plentiful in the UK. At Durrington Walls, walking distance from Stonehenge itself, there is evidence of two wood circles and a third known as Woodhenge, also aligned with the sun. Around this timber henge at Durrington, 5,000 years ago, there are thought to have been up to 1,000 people living in a settlement, which is clear evidence of the importance of these henges.

Seahenge, which re-emerged from the sea in 1998 off the east coast of Norfolk, is another example of a timber henge, thought to date back to 2049 BCE. The discovery led to more speculation about the rituals and uses associated with henges of both stone and wood, because in the middle of the circle of fifty-five wooden trunks is an upturned tree root that some have speculated was used in a similar way to the sky burials of Tibet. This is the practice of leaving a deceased person's body to nature, where the birds and animals will aid the process of decomposition. This ritual is not necessarily connected to the sun, but it certainly offers another example of the connection between the earth and the sky that these circles provide. Not only that, but in the case of Seahenge it is clear these peoples also created a link to the sea.

Whilst the solstice is one of the better-known names for the events at this time of year, another name used is Litha. This is the Old English name for the months of June and July. The Venerable Bede wrote, in his eighth-century work *The Reckoning of Time*, that Litha was also used to refer to the calm seas that were conducive to travel at this time of year.

Litha was a festival that involved the whole community and there are again countless examples of this festival across Europe. To celebrate Litha or midsummer, as it is also known, chains of bonfires are lit along the coasts of Cornwall and Northumberland. Professor Ronald Hutton, whom I have mentioned before, believes that this is a protection festival where blessings are sought by the community to help them through the long days of summer. He argues that with around seventeen hours of daylight at this time of year, there was increased danger for travellers in the form of highway robbery. For farmers there was a higher risk of cattle theft, and it also was a time when crops were at their tallest and so could easily be damaged by inclement weather.

Further south, in France, there was a tradition of rolling a wheel of fire down a hill. This was often a cartwheel or a straw wheel set on fire and rolled down an incline and into a lake or a pond to extinguish the fire. It is thought to have represented the coming of the dark half of the year as the sun, from this point on, will move closer to the horizon and eventually give way to the dark days of winter.

Wheels have long been associated with the sun, and in fact there is a Celtic god named Taranis who is often depicted holding a wheel and a lightning bolt. This clearly marks him out as a sky god with the lightning bolt also linking him to the sun.

Whilst these traditions surrounding the solstice sometimes have relatively modern roots, the megaliths thought to be associated with the sun have been here for thousands of years. In many cases we are not exactly sure how megaliths came to be, although we can get a good idea through experimental archaeology. Our ancestors were not so sure, however, and they created many stories about these monuments.

Often the stories and legends are anecdotal and lend themselves to telling around the dinner table or whilst you a supping a pint at the local hostelry. So rather than tell you one story about the standing stones of Britain, I have put together below a series of these little legends so that you may share them next time you are visiting one of these circles. You might even arrange a solstice feast for your friends and family, and tell a few of the stories then.

DANCING WITCHES, COWS AND KINGS: STORIES OF STANDING STONES

Dancing Witches

In Penrith in Cumbria there is a stone circle thought to be Neolithic in origin that is named 'Long Meg and Her Daughters'. William Wordsworth was noted to have commented that these stones were second only to Stonehenge. The legend goes that the stones, only twenty-seven of which remain standing to this day, were once a coven of witches. As punishment for dancing on the holy day of Sunday, a magician turned them to stone and made it impossible for them to be counted. If anyone is able to count them twice and come up with the same number on both counts, the curse will be lifted and the coven will return to its corporal form.

Long Meg is thought to have been Meg of Meldon, also known as Margaret Fenwick, a seventeenth-century woman referred to locally as a witch. This reputation may actually have been linked to her business as a moneylender and her opportune foreclosure on the loans she had made to two large estates, which brought her much wealth. Her prosperity was considered suspicious and her seizure of the properties was not at all popular with the landed gentry of the time, perhaps because she was a woman. I'll let you decide whether or not Meg was a witch or simply a shrewd businesswoman, but she is now thought to haunt the surrounding area as well as being linked to the standing stones at Penrith.

Castlerigg Stone Circle, again in Cumbria, this time just outside Keswick, is very popular with tourists and if you have the chance to visit you will see why. Looking south, Castlerigg Fell and High Rigg frame the circle, and if you look north you will see the mighty Skiddaw and Blencathra,

STORIES OF THE SUN

Skiddaw being the sixth-highest mountain in the UK. This circle is thought to be older than Stonehenge and also has the folklore motif of 'countless stones' associated with it. In this case, if you manage to count the same number of standing stones twice, you have achieved the impossible and who knows what will occur next?

Zealous Brides

More dancing on the Sabbath resulted in mishap in Stanton Drew in Somerset. There are three stone circles in Stanton Drew in close proximity to each other; one large and two small. Why they were built this way almost 5,000 years ago, no one knows, but one story tells of a wedding party. It was a Saturday evening and the happy couple were celebrating at their wedding reception and all their guests danced well into the night. The moon rose high and the fiddler's music rang out across the countryside. But come midnight, when the church bells took over to mark the start of a new day, Sunday, the fiddler stopped and refused to play any more.

The bride tried every which way to get the fiddler to play again, but he would play on the Sabbath for neither love nor money. Eventually she shouted at him that she would go to hell before she would stop dancing and with that the Devil appeared from the ground, fiddle in hand, and started to play for the bride, her groom and the assembled guests.

Well, they danced once more and whether they were able to stop, had they wanted to, no one knows, but as the cockerel crowed and the sun rose, every single one of the wedding party gathered in the fields turned to stone.

Dancing on the Sabbath is a recurring theme when it comes to the origin stories of some of the 1,000 stone circles across the UK and there are many more to tell, including the Nine Maidens Stone Circle on Dartmoor, but let's go now to the time of King Arthur where we find the legend of Stonehenge and how it came into being.

The Magician that Moved Stone

In *The History of the Kings of Britain*, Geoffrey of Monmouth talks of how the great magician of Arthurian legend, Merlin, was summoned by Aurelius to solve the problem of creating a place of memorial for the fallen warriors of Salisbury after Hengist turned on them. Merlin suggested moving what he refers to as 'The Giant's Ring', situated in Ireland, and placing it near Salisbury in order to create a burial ground for those they had lost. Aurelius laughed at him at first, stating that there was no way such stones could be moved such a distance. But Merlin insisted there was a way.

Aurelius then tasked Arthur (Utherpendragon), 15,000 men and Merlin with the job of retrieving the stones from Mount Killaraus in Ireland. In the battle that followed, the Irish were defeated easily and Merlin and the men arrived at the stones. After a few false starts where Arthur's men attempted to move the stones by the usual means of ropes and wooden logs, Merlin stepped in and the stones were moved under his magical supervision across the sea to just outside Salisbury. This is how Stonehenge came to be.

Seven Steps to a Kingdom

Another story connected with kings and standing stones concerns the Rollright Stones in Oxfordshire. A king, intent on conquering England, was striding across the land with his army when he encountered a woman, often described as a witch. She made him aware of her power and told him that if he could walk seven paces across the earth and was able to view the village some way off down in the valley in front of him, she would ensure that he became King of England. Enthused by this idea and sure he would succeed, the king took seven strides and, as he was about to complete the seventh stride, he and all his men turned to stone. To this day the tallest stone is known as the King's Stone, just outside the village of Long Compton.

Waste Not, Want Not

As well as witches and kings, there are some standing stone stories that tell of magical cows. It is one such story that is held in the legend of Mitchell's Fold. It is told that there was a magical cow that had been gifted to the once-starving community of Stapley Hill in Shropshire. The cow was able to give the villagers an infinite supply of milk on the one condition that they only took a pail a day each and no more.

A local witch decided she would bring further misery to the village by wasting the milk of the magic cow. She walked up to the hill where the cow was grazing and milked it through a sieve, so that the milk ran down the hill unused. When the cow realised what she was doing, it turned on the witch, kicking her in the chest and turning her into a stone. The witch still stands there today and the surrounding stones are referred to as her followers, although they do not play a part in this tale.

There is a similar tale associated with the standing stones at Calanais on the island of Lewis in the Outer Hebrides.

This theme of a witch stealing milk fits in with the folk-lore surrounding the Mjölkhare of Scandinavia, which is thought to be a witch transformed into a hare, or simply the witch's familiar that steals milk from the cows, leaving them dry and ailing.

The motif of the magic cow with infinite milk sustaining nations also fits with Auðumbla, the cow who brings forth rivers of milk in the Norse creation myth, and Hathor, a solar goddess from Egyptian mythology who is often depicted as a cow with the sun between her horns.

Balor with the Evil Eye

Come with me to Ireland where there are more magical cows and a myth thought to be a legend associated with the creation of Rockabill Islands.

In the time of the Tuatha Dé Dannan, there was a magic cow named Glas Gaibhneann that gave forth an infinite supply of milk. The one-eyed Formorian king and giant Balor, with the power to turn anything to stone with a glance from his eye, coveted this cow and sent a servant to retrieve it and its calf. Balor told the servant that he must under no circumstances let the cow's calf fall behind or the cow would turn to look for it and will see that it had been led away from its homeland.

The servant managed the majority of this journey without mishap, until they reached a river and the calf fell behind. The cow turned to find the calf and saw her home on the horizon. She let out a mighty below of anguish, which Balor heard.

As Balor turned to see what had happened, he forgot to close his eye. He turned the cow and her calf to stone, and it is these stones that are said to have created Rockabill Island.

Balor is also associated with the sun, as his eye opening is said to be akin to the rising of the sun. There are two standing stones at Baltray that are aligned with the sun, perhaps Balor's eye, rising above Rockabill Islands.

So you see, dancers, witches, cows and kings seem to be inextricably linked to our sun and the stories of standing stones.

SOLAR WHEEL WREATH

Over the last decade, door wreaths have grown in popularity. For over 100 years they have appeared on our doors at Christmas, but we now see seasonal wreaths throughout the year, adorning doorways. As you might expect, wreaths are particularly popular during the autumn and winter months with many places offering wreath-making workshops.

The summer solstice sits directly opposite the winter solstice, so for this chapter I am inviting you to create a solar wheel wreath for your home or front door. You don't need anything particularly fancy to do this, but here are some basics, and if you are stuck for ideas, I have gathered some examples on the website page that accompanies this book. You will find the web address in the introduction.

You Will Need

A circular frame: these are often available in craft shops, or you can try making your own – there are several 'how to' videos available online if you search for them. They are usually made out of willow, metal or wicker, and it's entirely up to you what size you use.

Floristry wire, wool or string: these will make good ties as you need something to tie your items onto the wreath frame. It's better to use a natural fibre of some kind and not cable ties if at all possible.

Decorations:

Coloured raffia

Coloured wool

Flowers – from the garden or shop bought, real or artificial

Origami flowers

Feathers

Beads

Ribbon

Scissors and glue: you will need scissors to cut items to the shape or length you want them to be and maybe even secateurs if you are cutting plants from the garden. A hot glue gun is often useful for attaching items that can't necessarily be tied to the wreath, but I try to avoid this as much as possible.

How to Make Your Wreath

If you haven't got a pre-made wreath frame, you could try making one from green hazel or willow.

Gather together the items you want to make your wreath with and cut some lengths of string or wire, whichever you are using, to tie them to your wreath.

Take your wreath frame and wind the raffia, ribbons or wool around the hoop until the wreath is covered. Use different colours, perhaps yellows, oranges, reds and golds, to represent the sun, or the pinks, peaches and lilacs of the dawn.

When you have wrapped the whole of the wreath, secure the end of the covering with a piece of wire, string or glue to stop it unravelling.

Gather the larger items you are decorating the wreath with, such as flowers or feathers in small bunches or arrangements that can be tied together. Roses are plentiful at this time of year along with oxeye daisies and sunflowers. Fresh herbs are also a nice idea and will make your wreath smell wonderful. Fennel, lavender and mint are seasonal favourites.

Once you've created enough small bunches of decorations to cover the wreath, or as many as you would like if you don't want to cover the whole hoop, tie them to the wreath, overlapping each other slightly and working your way clockwise around the whole circle from the top middle.

Once your wreath is covered, you can then embellish it by securing beads, origami flowers or whatever takes your fancy with a little dab of hot glue or, better still, a needle and thread.

To hang your wreath, use a piece of string looped around the top or place it on a mantelpiece or shelf. Stand back and admire.

The above is just a suggestion and you can create whatever design you would like in whatever way the solstice inspires you. To make a Celtic sun wheel, you could place two sticks in a cross behind the circle of the wreath so that they intersect the wreath from top to bottom, left to right. You could create plaits of wool that hang from the bottom of the wreath to represent the rays of the sun. You could even make your wreath into a centrepiece for a solstice supper.

JULY

KEEPERS OF THE SUN

IT'S 4.30 A.M. AND SUNRISE this morning is at 5.03 a.m., rising in the north-east. We are in the middle of a heatwave in the UK and it is already 16°C, even though the sun is nowhere to be seen. I no longer need my ski trousers and layers of thermals. Jeans and a t-shirt are all that is required. The first thing I notice on the way out is how little birdsong there is. The roofs are practically silent compared to three months ago.

The sky is translucent blue and scattered with cirrocumulus clouds. To the east behind me is a yellow glow as I walk west to my spot on the far hill.

In the tree-arched alley, the burgeoning branches spill forth from gardens, enormous fat fig-tree leaves beside needle-thin pine. Bugles of convolvulus flowers twist along the path and the birds burst sliently from the undergrowth. I am walking quite briskly as I am a little later than I would have liked to be. I have time but the birds sense I am on a mission. Their usual tutting is absent as, after weeks of bringing up their young, they don't have the strength. Frankly they just want to lie down in a dark hawthorn. I empathise.

The wispy silk threads of cobwebs on my face tell me I'm the first to come through here this morning. Arachne's careful work is gone in a second. A break in the trees gives me a glimpse of the orange skyline and the mowed meadow that encompasses my sit-spot.

A persistent mewing buzzard interrupts my thoughts. A young one, perhaps just fledged, still hoping its parents will feed it. Beneath me the roots of trees stretch like finger bones across the path. To the other side of me rabbits scurry away. I can hear deer ahead and I spot a flash of their white rumps; bright apostrophes in the just-dark wood. As I reach the edge of the wood to turn into the field, I finally hear some familiar voices. Song thrush, wren and pigeon.

Dark magenta-edged clouds drift across the horizon, and as I approach my sit-spot, walking over the gently undulating field, the heads of six or seven blackbirds appear from the dewy grass, hunting for insects. They see me coming and move off, silently.

With the grass mown short, there is plenty of choice for places to sit this morning and I sit on the ridge a few feet from the footpath that runs along the edge of the woodland.

Above me, a pigeon does an impressive Tom Daley-style dive out of the tree and, as I settle in, the blackbirds go back to their insect hunt in the dip just below where I sit.

The clouds are going from pink to orange and eventually there is the particular shade of yellow glow I have come to associate with the imminent arrival of the sun. I check my watch. Three minutes to sun up. A pair of jays argue, dancing around in the large oak tree behind me.

I sit for a while and let my ears adjust to the sounds of the morning. I am perplexed by a bird's song that sounds like a strange mix of blackbird and swallow. Later I discover this is a black cap, which most likely I have not heard before due to the weight of the dawn chorus earlier in the year.

I hear some blundering about in the woods off to the left of me and my buck buddy tumbles out of the wood to eat the dew-laden grass in the meadow. He doesn't notice me at first. I watch him through binoculars to see if I can learn a little more about him before he spots me.

I note he has a greying face, which there is a special word for in German. *Muffelfleck* translates as 'muffle stain' and it shows that he's older than his behaviour suggests. His broad back and stocky neck echo this. He knows me this time and doesn't bark; instead he steps forward confidently, older and wiser. I continue to watch him through the binoculars and he moves forward another few feet. I lower my binoculars and ask if he'd like to join me. He steps forward again and for a moment I think he might actually be about to join me, and then he thinks better of it, leaping away back to the edge of the wood, following it along until he finds his usual desire path. Mid-July to mid-August is the rutting season, so perhaps he was just trying to work out if I am still a threat, although I like to think he and I recognise each other after seven months of sunrises.

The sun is full in the sky and blinding. The road below in the village is now busy with people going to work. Monday morning is gearing up and a person walking their dog appears on the footpath. I look at my watch, 5.45 a.m. – time to move on.

As I walk back through the wood, fat sycamore keys litter the path, and once I am back down into the village, I hear young swifts screaming as they have their first flying lessons. It's a heart-warming moment to witness, especially as for the first four years of their life, these young ones will not stop flying.

The sun's rays now flood the street I walk along and I cannot look straight ahead, it's so bright. In its morning colours, there is no denying the power of the sun. Its golden aesthetic has represented power and opulence for thousands of years.

For the ancient Egyptians, the king was the personification of the sun. This belief reached its zenith with what is referred to as Atenism, introduced by Amenhotep IV. It was considered that the king during this time was the manifestation of the sun and responsible for maintaining good relations between humans and the sun god Ra. Amenhotep ruled Egypt for twenty years and was a divisive character. He moved the Egyptian religion to monotheism rather than polytheism and the single god he chose was Ra the sun god, or Aten as he was also known during this time. As part of his new regime, he rebuilt the capital city and attempted to remove any previous art, writing and records of deities that were not Ra or symbolic of Aten. The new city is what is now known as Tell el Amarna. Amenhotep also renamed himself Akhenaten and this new name translated as someone who was working on behalf of Aten.

When Akhenaten died this new religion was almost entirely reversed and the Egyptian deities preceding Akhenaten's reign were worshipped once more. However,

Ra still retained his significance within the pantheon. Even before Akhenaten, Egyptians believed that the sun was the source of all creation and had spontaneously appeared at the beginning of time.

To explain this miracle of creation, the Egyptians looked to the dung beetle. The image of the dung beetle encasing its eggs in dung and then rolling the dung up into a huge ball, until finally the larvae hatch, eat the dung and emerge as fully formed adult beetles, was for them the perfect analogy for the fertility and power of the sun. In fact, the scarab beetle came to be used as a solar amulet in many cases. Furthermore, the pushing of the dung along the earth's surface, to the Egyptians, represented the journey of the sun across the sky each day.

Ra, like several other sun gods, steers a solar ship across the sky every day. There are two celestial boats in Egyptian mythology: Mandjet, the boat of the day, and Mesektet, the boat of the night. The crew of the boats varied in number but Ra invariably has a retinue. The journeys of both these boats were mapped out using the twelve sections of the clock, referred to in the March chapter. At one point there were also religious recitals ascribed to these twelve sections of the day.

Academics are not quite sure exactly where the number of hours came from, but one theory proffered is that this twelve-section framework was perhaps offered up by the observation that the moon completes its cycle of phases twelve times within the turning of the four seasons, and that this also marked one cycle of the sun from south-east to north-east.

Ancient Mesopotamians also linked their kings with the sun and believed that the king drew his power from it. They were able to predict eclipses of the sun, and if the king was advised of an eclipse, a decoy king was placed on the throne.

It was this decoy king's job to offer himself as a sacrifice to the sun gods in place of the king. The king himself would hide until the danger had passed.

For the Aztecs the sun's journey across the sky actually meant it personified different gods as it travelled. The god Tonatiuh was the sun by day and was hauled into the sky by warriors who had died in battle and whose souls had become hummingbirds for this task. A fire serpent named Xiucóatl then led Tonatiuh across the sky until at noon he became Huitzilopovhtli, the god who defeated all darkness. When the sun set, it was the Cilhuateteo who pulled the sun towards the earth. The Cilhuateteo were the souls of women who had died in childbirth.

For the Egyptians it was Ra in his sun boat, for the Aztecs it was souls, but for others it was a chariot that transported the sun from one side of the sky to the other. In the Greek Pantheon, Helios has a chariot pulled by four horses across the sky. In the Norse creation story, Sol the daughter of Mundilfari (god of time) is the goddess who drives a chariot that holds the sun, with the wolf Sköll in pursuit. I have mentioned Sol before and I will talk more about Sol and Sköll in the last chapter.

Elsewhere in Indo-European mythology, we find the divine twins who are sometimes two separate deities working together and at other times a dual-headed warrior. The deity is usually the daughter or goddess of the sun and, again, pulls a chariot that holds the sun. When she is pulled beneath the water, by either serpents or a dragon, night falls and, during this phase of the sun's journey, the divine twins are represented as human brothers or horses, who dive beneath the water and guide the chariot through the underworld.

Further evidence of these sun chariots can be found in the Trundholm Sun Chariot, which was discovered in 1902 in

Trundholm, Denmark, in what remained of old marshland. It is a Bronze Age statuette that depicts a divine horse pulling the sun in a chariot. Historians and archaeologists have suggested that the statue was used by Bronze Age priests to demonstrate and celebrate the movement of the sun across the sky each day.

As we can see from the Trundholm find, it wasn't just gods and kings that were the keepers of the sun, charged with ensuring the correct rituals were performed in order for it to make its daily journey across the sky. In different cultures, priests, druids and bards also held the rituals, knowledge and words to complete these tasks.

In the case of the famous Milesian bard Amergin, when the Milesians and their king arrived in Ireland, he stepped off the boat at Inbher Culpa and announced, in what is generally known as 'The Song of Amergin':

> Who else knows the ages of the moon?
> Who else knows where the sunset settles?
> Who else knows the secrets of the unhewn dolmen?
>
> From 'The Song of Amergin', translated by Michael R. Burch

Shortly after this the Milesians discovered that the Tuatha Dé Danann were already in residence in Ireland. The Tuatha Dé Danann informed the Milesians that their arrival and announcement that they would take the land as their own was unchivalrous, and that the Milesians should have given the Tuatha Dé Danann more notice of their arrival in order that they might defend themselves.

Amergin was then given the job of deciding whether or not this was so, and he decided in favour of the Tuatha Dé Danann. The Milesians got back on their boats and anchored out at sea before returning at an allotted time and eventually defeating the Tuatha Dé Danann. During this battle, Amergin is said to have fought and killed Mac Gréine, who worshipped and kept the sun within the Tuatha Dé Danann.

Whether this story is historical fact, legend or part of the Celtic mythology is not known, but it is thought that the characters may be based on real events and that their stories are exaggerated for theatrical effect.

The world over, there is evidence of the worship of the sun and the tools, ceremonial wear and adornments of those who led and facilitated this worship. This includes the amulets and headdresses found in the ancient tombs of Egypt and, in the UK, the many archaeological finds that show the Celtic peoples wore symbols of the sun.

Golden lunulae, named because of their crescent moon shape, are thought to have been worn by those wishing to worship the sun. These were golden, flat, crescent-shaped, engraved pieces worn around the neck and would have been made by the most skilled of goldsmiths.

Sun discs were often worn as brooches and the motifs within this jewellery were representative of the position of the sun at certain times of day or year. High-status individuals would have most likely worn these pieces of solar art and they gave the wearer protection and imbued them with the very power of the sun. In some cases, the discs may have been sewn onto clothing and identified the wearer as a pilgrim of the sun, perhaps visiting Stonehenge each year for the solstices.

A find in Bern, Switzerland shows how people may have used these solar symbols for protection or to represent the authority of the wearer. The artefact is thought to be a prosthetic limb dating from the Bronze Age and takes the form of a bronze hand with a gold cuff. Etched into the gold cuff are symbols attributed to the sun, suggesting the wearer was someone of importance.

Larger items of goldware have been discovered, such as pieces that sat across the shoulders like a solid cape and pointed pyramidal hats that are almost 1m tall. These may have been worn by the priests and priestesses as they carried out the rituals to worship the sun. Some of these hats are covered in symbols thought to represent the universe and the sun, and they were found in burial sites separate from any one person's grave, suggesting that they were community-owned objects rather than the property of one individual.

That evening as I watch the hazy sunset from my loft room window, I see a doe and her two kids wander into the freshly cut meadow to delight in the new hay, and there is a symmetry to my day in the deer, the sun and the fields. I have watched the sun rise and set, noted the company it keeps, and my cup of yellow camomile tea pays homage to the sun as it rests for another day.

THE SUN'S STORY IN PICTURES

Artefacts found in Denmark dating to 1150–750 BCE tell the story of the sun and its keepers via carvings on tiny razors in the shape of boats. Hundreds of these razors have been found across Scandinavia, not in sets but as individual vignettes of the story, and archaeologist Flemming Kaul's studies have led to the conclusion that these razors and the images on them relate to the journey of the sun each day. When placed together, they indicate the belief that at various points in the sun's journey, different animals take custody of it. This story was displayed as an animation as part of the British Museum's Stonehenge exhibition.

The pictures represent sunrise as a fish dragging the sun from the sea and onto the bow of a boat. A bird then clasps the sun in its feet and carries it into the sky, and when it tires a galloping horse takes over, leaping up into the heavens with the sun on its back until the orb reaches its zenith. The horse then delivers the sun safely back onto the bow of the boat, which continues its journey over the water. Finally, from under the water a sea serpent rises to take the sun back beneath the waves and into the underworld.

Curator Jennifer Wexler of the British Museum suggests that in this story the sun rises and sets in the sea because much of Scandinavia is surrounded by the sea. Therefore, it would have appeared to the peoples of these lands that the sun was travelling over the land during the day and then under the sea at night.

There are echoes of this pictorial sun story in that of the Egyptian night boat that would have been told perhaps 1,500 years before. This time the boat travels underground at night, as opposed to under the sea. Perhaps, then, this is one of those stories that has travelled and became part of the collective consciousness. Whether the story came from one root and travelled through oral storytelling (monogenesis), or popped up in a variety of different cultures as a very human interpretation of the sun (polygenesis), it is nevertheless a story we are very familiar with, and so here is my interpretation of the story of the great god Ra.

THE JOURNEY OF THE GREAT GOD RA

Ra is a mighty god. He rules all. What lies above, what lies below and all that lies in between. Keeper of the sun, each morning the falcon-headed, warrior god throws open the golden gates of the sky.

As he does, the boat Mandjet is waiting for him to alight. Covered in precious gems, crystals and gold, this boat shines like the sun it holds in its hull. It begins its journey across the sky with Ra and his warriors at the helm. Sailing east to west, the light they hold shines down on the earth below.

Mandjet and its crew eventually complete their arc across the heavens, but their journey does not end there for now they must take the dangerous journey through the underworld, Duat.

Here the boat becomes known as Mesektet and it knows not a moment's peace as it is hunted by the beings that dwell in the land of the dead.

Mythical creatures, serpents and reptiles live here but none are as fearsome as Apep, an enormous sea snake that hounds the boat emitting thunderous roars, which shake the land beneath the earth and threaten to upturn the boat.

Apep tries time and time again to take the sun from Ra and his crew. But with the great god Ra overseeing the warriors, the serpent's attempts to swallow the glowing orb are thwarted and eventually they emerge from the underworld in time for Ra to throw open the gates of the sky once more.

SUN AMULET

Mala beads have become very popular in recent years, particularly in yogic practice. It's important to note that malas are from the Hindu religion and what makes them malas is that they have 108 beads and 1 large guru bead. They are used for meditation, prayer and for repeating a mantra. Prayer beads have, however, been in use for thousands of years in a variety of cultures.

The word 'bead' in the English language is thought to be derived from the Anglo-Saxon word *bede*, meaning 'bid', as in to be bidden to pray.

These necklaces can provide comfort and reassurance. They make great tools for meditation and mindfulness practices. For this activity you are invited to create a mala that celebrates the sun, using beads of citrine and carnelian with some accent beads of your choice and a guru stone of your choice. Malas are traditionally made from rudraksha seeds, but they can be made of many different types of beads.

In my version of this necklace, I used a scarab beetle charm, which sits at the back of the neck, to represent the Egyptian mythology and ancient Egyptians' belief that the dung or scarab beetle, as it pushed its ball of dung across the surface of the earth, represented the passage of the sun. Essentially all you need is strong, thin cord, 108 beads of the same size and 1 larger guru bead and a tassel.

If you are in need of inspiration, you can find a picture of the mala I made on the website page that accompanies this book. You will also find an example of how to make a mala via the video links there. You will find the web address for this page in the introduction.

If you would like to create this mala, you will need the supplies detailed below, but please feel free to choose your own colours and themes.

Once you have completed your mala, you could use it with the Blue Sky meditation track provided for you on the website page and detailed in August's chapter.

You Will Need

1.5m of 0.4mm waxed linen cord
1 × 1.5mm-diameter crimp bead
1 × small jump ring
1 × 8mm red agate or carnelian guru bead
46 × 6mm citrine beads
48 × 6mm carnelian beads
14 × accent beads
1 × silk yellow tassel with a metal cap and loop
1 × scarab beetle charm or similar
Fine round-nose pliers
Scissors

How to Make Your Sun Amulet

Cut a piece of cord approximately 1.5m long. This is likely to be more than you need, but this is to allow for mistakes.

Fold the cord in half by taking the two ends of the cord and placing them together.

Take the looped end and feed it through the loop in the top of the tassel's cap. Then feed the opposite two ends of the cord through the looped end of the cord and pull tight.

Thread the two loose ends of the cord through your larger, guru bead.

Holding the two ends together, loop them around your fingers and knot as close to the guru bead as possible. You may find using a pair of fine round-nose pliers helps to get the knots tight to the beads.

Divide the rest of your beads into two groups of 54.

Lay them out in the order in which you want to thread them onto the cord.

Start with one of the strands of cord (one side of the necklace) and thread your first bead on.

Again, knot as close to the bead as possible before adding the next bead.

Continue until you have threaded and knotted on all 54 beads.

Repeat for the other side of the necklace, using the second strand of cord.

Once both sides are strung with beads, you can knot the two ends together.

You can secure the knots with a dab of hot glue or a crimp bead.

Next take the jump ring and open it up using the pliers.

Loop on your chosen charm and then close the jump ring around the crimp bead or knot at the back of the necklace.

You should now have a completed necklace.

AUGUST

DOG DAYS

LIGHT SEEPS UNDER THE PLEATS of the thin cur-
tains of the holiday cottage and I do not need an alarm to
wake me. I am in an unfamiliar place and so more sensitive
to its rhythms, which differ from that of the downs. We are
staying beside the River Tees, in Wycliffe, County Durham.

It's 4 a.m. and the sun is raring to go. I boil a milk-pan of water on the glowing electric stove to make my obligatory coffee. The house is silent but for the tick of the kitchen clock. The water hisses, I turn off the stove and the red glow fades. I pour out my coffee and walk out to the little bank-side garden through a glorious boot room. Boot rooms are another of those liminal spaces. A space between the outside world and domesticity. A place where mud can dwell with impunity on the bottom of boots, where raincoats can drip and dogs can shake their coats dry. I have neither a boot room nor a dog, but I feel sure that if I had a boot room, a dog would quickly follow.

Outside I sit on a greying wooden garden bench. A crescent moon hangs in a cornflower-blue sky. To the left of me is the River Tees. Collections of rocks create mini rapids in the water, a bit further up the river in front of me and down the river behind me. The juxtaposition of mirror-still water and washing machine turbulence so close together is a wonder of nature. On the opposite bank is a hanger of trees straining to touch the surface of the river without falling in.

Trees are vital for riverbanks. They help to soak up rain run-off from the earth beside the rivers, which can pollute the watercourses. They provide shade from the sun and, of course, they are an essential ecosystem for a variety of flora and fauna.

On my side of the bank, just below the bench where I am sitting, I hear the distinctive plop of a water vole. I scan the bank, knowing that there is little hope of seeing this secretive creature in amongst the busy foliage of summer, but instead I spot the wych elm leaning into the river.

The wych elm can grow up to 40m tall, so this one on the bank is quite small. This magical tree has become one of my favourites. In woodlands in the spring, its leaves rival the beech trees in their luminescence. Their winged fruit, known as samara, hang like tiny wedding bouquets in the spring, easily parted from their branches to fling themselves at potential future brides. There is no fruit left on this one. Their leaves are easily confused with hazel leaves, which explains its other name, wych hazel.

It has in fact many other names, one of which is the elven tree as it is thought that elves dwell there and that these particular elves guard the souls of the dead and ensure their safe passage to the underworld. Perhaps because of this, elm is often the choice of wood for coffins.

In folklore some carry a small piece of it for protection as it is said to repel witches, although the wych in the name is not a reference to this. Instead, the word signals the malleable nature of the elm tree and its wood.

The familiar pre-dawn glow is present above the treeline where the river starts to disappear around a bend. I have not been out here long when I discover I have not brought enough warm clothes with me for this task. I lived in Durham for a large chunk of my life, but I have now lived in the south-east for much longer than I ever lived here and I have gone soft. It is 6°C – 5 degrees cooler than it would be in my sit-spot back home. The sunrise is also eleven minutes earlier, reminding me, once more, that it's all about the angle.

In the river, fish jump to catch the early morning midges, and above the rush of the river rapids, I can just about hear wrens, pigeons and blackbirds in the treeline opposite, but they all remain well hidden.

It is then I hear another call above them; one I've not heard for a long time – the peep-peep of a kingfisher. I scan the bank in the half-light and I am rewarded with a flash of turquoise lightning as it flits across the river.

Halcyon is the Latin name for the kingfisher and the phrase 'halcyon days' refers to a time when things are perfect, blissful or utopian. You might even use it to refer to the warm sunlit days of summer, yet what it actually refers to is fourteen days during midwinter.

In the Greek myth of Halcyon and Ceyx, the two were so in love that they thought nothing could touch them. On occasion, they even called themselves Zeus and Hera, which of course angered the actual Zeus and Hera. Ceyx was the protector of sailors, sheltering them from storms at sea, and so as punishment for their vanity Zeus sent a storm to drown Ceyx. So strong was their love that a distraught Halcyon drowned herself so that she might join Ceyx. The gods were moved by this turn of events and they turned the lovers into kingfishers.

But what about those halcyon days? The Greeks believed that kingfishers nested in the midwinter, way out at sea, laying their eggs on rafts of twigs. It was believed that in sympathy for Halcyon and Ceyx, each year the gods would calm the waters for seven days either side of the winter solstice in order to allow Halcyon to incubate her eggs. This belief is also noted in the work of the Roman author Pliny. He writers that as long as the kingfisher is sitting on her eggs, there will be no storms at sea.

Unwilling as I am to break the magic of this myth, the kingfisher actually nests in the early spring, as you might expect for a bird familiar with the climate of the UK. During this time a kingfisher can catch over 100 fish a day in order to feed the seven hungry mouths it may have in its bankside nest.

Further up the river is a group of eight goosanders. Behind them a grey heron lands silently and begins to fish off the edge of a spit of rocks that jut out from the bank on the other side. The jetty of flat rocks reaches a good two thirds across the river, providing an excellent spot for resting, gossiping, preening and, of course, fishing. It's far enough away that the birds don't bother about my presence, but close enough that I have the great pleasure of watching them in their early morning routines.

While I'm watching all this activity, a bluetit or titmouse, as Gilbert White refers to them in his journals, joins me in the garden. It hops amongst the dog roses searching for drowsy insects still cold from the night.

Six loud brent geese fly overhead, announcing the arrival of the sun as it pushes up over the trees. The kingfisher peep-peeps and shoots back across the river, rusty-bellied, feathers iridescent in the first rays of sun. It twists and turns, showing me turquoise and brick red, and leaving me in no doubt, even without binoculars, that this is my halcyon friend.

Finally, the sun is high enough and warm enough to begin to thaw my numb hands and I feel a primal need to turn my face towards it, close my eyes and soak up its rays.

The first dog walkers start to appear on the spit of stones opposite and I am brought back to my thoughts on the boot room and wet dogs. Over the next half hour more dog walkers appear as the sun climbs higher and I am reminded of the phrase 'dog days', used to refer to the very hottest days of summer.

In 2021 the UK had the ninth hottest summer on record, and in the year when I sat beside the river, 2022, August was the third hottest ever in Europe. In the UK we had an exceptional heatwave where temperatures reached over 40°C in some places. In fact, 2022 was noted by the Met Office as the warmest year on record in the UK. We are noticing that our 'dog days' are getting hotter and our weather is becoming more extreme. There can be no denying the climate crisis when faced with summer temperatures like this in the UK.

The phrase 'dog days' originates from the Latin *dies canicu-lares*. Romans believed that the because the dog star (Sirius, in the constellation Canis Major) appears bright in the sky beside the rising sun, between July and August, when some of the hottest days in the year occur, the dog star must be somehow adding to the sun's heat. The heat of these days was thought to be the cause of increased irrational and odd behaviour during this time.

The Romans weren't the only culture to associate the sun with dogs of some kind, as there are several dog-headed or dog-associated gods and goddesses, throughout the world, which are also connected to the sun.

Hecate is a Greek goddess who appears in many stories. She is often depicted as carrying a torch of fire and walking dogs. In some depictions she has three heads, those of a serpent, a horse and a dog, and her cloak is the colour of gold. She is often referred to as the goddess of the night, yet her gold cloak and the torch of fire could be argued to represent the light of the sun, so she is still occasionally referred to as a goddess of the sun. This is the subject of much debate and has led to some proffering the theory that she is a sky goddess rather than a goddess of night or day. Even her origins are shrouded in mystery. Some theorise that she came from Anatolia and was indeed a sun goddess; others, that she evolved from an Egyptian frog goddess responsible for fertility and childbirth. It's easy to see how all these ingredients in the pot could lead to the prevailing modern thought of Hecate as a goddess of witchcraft.

The Aztecs also had a dog-headed god associated with the sun. Interestingly, this god is also associated with the underworld – the above and below of the sun's journey represented in one god. This also echoes dog gods of other mythologies, such as Cerberus, the many-headed dog guardian of the underworld in the Greek pantheon, and Anubis, the guider of the dead, in the Egyptian.

Most of the information we have about the Aztec culture comes from after the conquests. The Spanish conquistadors taught young indigenous peoples how to read and write in Spanish, and therefore these histories are occasionally skewed to favour the employer. For example, they would not have called themselves Aztecs, that's the Spanish name for them. One of the ways they referred to themselves was as the Mexica (Me-shee-ka), which is where the name Mexico comes from.

They were a complex and advanced society that is thought to have been established around the thirteenth century. That's at about the same time as people in Britain were fighting amongst themselves, with Henry III emerging from the fray. Their main city, Tenochtitlan, was the centre of their society; a society that spread out to cover an area the size of Britain.

Mexica society was based on collaboration and community. Everyone played their part. You were given land to work in order to provide food for your family and wider community, but if you did not work that land for over a year, the land was taken back and given to another who would work it for the good of Mexica society.

Of course, the Mexica had their own language and methods of recording, but the codices (illuminated manuscripts) that we get most of our knowledge from today were written by Spanish chroniclers or by the indigenous peoples taught to read and write in Spanish and employed by the aforementioned chroniclers. The most significant of these codices is considered to be the Codex Mendoza, thought to have been recorded in the mid-1500s for the Spanish king Charles V.

In these codices we find stories of Xolotl, a dog-headed god from the Mexica pantheon who is seen as the god of fire, lightning and death. Xolotl accompanies the sun through the Aztec nine-levelled underworld, Mictlán, protecting it from the rulers of Mictlán and delivering the souls of the dead to their final resting place. Xolotl has a twin brother, Quetzalcoatl, who brings the sun into the world every day, and Xolotl guides the sun at night.

As we saw in the previous chapter, for thousands of years humans watched the sun disappear below the horizon each day, not knowing that it disappeared because the earth was turning. It took the likes of Galileo to bring this to light. Instead, they theorised that it disappeared into the sea or an underworld of some kind. And so it is that the sun's connection with the underworld has endured within our myths. Dog-headed gods and goddesses, sacred hounds and sentinel canines all guard not just the dead but also, each night, the sun.

As we know from the history books, the Spanish were most interested in the Mexica's excess of gold. The Mexica were a bartering society and gold was part of that, but it was in such abundance that it was referred to by them as the faeces of the sun. It was also used in medicine, particularly in a tonic that could cure haemorrhoids or pustules on the skin, as these illnesses were linked to Nanahuatzin, a pustule-covered god who martyred himself and became the sun. It is his story, and that on the fifth era of creation in the Mexica's mythology, that I would like to share with you next.

XOLOTL, PROTECTOR OF THE SUN

The Aztec mythologies and creation stories are complex and nuanced and it's important to note that these stories were recorded, in the main, by colonialists. When telling this story, I have taken time to research the Mexica culture and its mythologies through books, podcasts and visits to museums. I have interpreted the story in a way that I hope represents it in the most authentic way possible.

There are several eras of the sun and creation in the mythologies. This story is of the creation of the fifth era, which is the era we are living in today.

The fourth era of creation was ending. The fourth sun had been destroyed and the gods of the ancient Mexica empire knew that in order for the fifth era to dawn, sacrifices must be made. A great fire was lit and the gods gathered together to decide who would make this sacrifice in order to rebirth the sun.

Most of the gods held back, not wanting to forfeit their life. Tēcciztēcatl, the snail god, saw the peril the world was in, stepped forward and offered himself. But Tēcciztēcatl was very rich and noble, and the other gods considered him too important to sacrifice. They began to persuade him that a lesser god should be given up.

Nanahuatzin knew of whom they were speaking. Covered in boils and with not a penny to his name, he knew what the other gods were thinking. He also knew that the world depended on him to show them what it was to be humble, so while the others argued he rushed forward and threw himself into the flames before Tēcciztēcatl could stop him. Proud Tēcciztēcatl was not about to be upstaged by Nanahuatzin, so he too threw himself into the fire.

Now the gods had two suns and they knew that two celestial bodies in the same sky could not coexist in peace. So, they took up a rabbit and hurled it at Tēcciztēcatl so that he became the moon, and if you look, he is forever with a rabbit upon his face.

The gods waited for the sun and the moon to start moving around the earth once more, but they did not. There came the realisation that in order to create the motion needed to move the orbs around the earth, they must all sacrifice themselves.

One by one the gods jumped into the fire, knowing that this was the only way to ensure the future of the earth. If any were hesitant or unsure, the god of the wind, Ehécatl, blew them into the fire. The only god to resist was Xolotl, who cried so hard that his eyes washed away.

Seeing that it would soon be his turn, he started to run. First, he used his powers to disguise himself as a double-stemmed maize plant, which we now know as xolotl. But this did not hide him for long, as Ehécatl blew through the maize flattening it, and Xolotl had to run once more.

This time he became an agave plant, which is now known as mexolotl. This did not work either, so Xolotl sought the shelter of the water and jumped into the river, turning himself into an amphibious salamander, the axolotl.

But the water could not save him and he was plucked from the river and blown into the fire by Ehécatl, who then followed him into the flames. At last, the gods had completed their task and the sun and the moon began to orbit once more, bringing life to the fifth era.

You may think that this was the end of Xolotl, but it is said that in the dawning of the new era he found a new role as he and his twin brother, Quetzalcoatl, travelled to the underworld to collect the bones that created humankind. Xolotl now bears the head of a dog and guides the dead to their final resting place. With his flaming torch he can fly to the heavens as lightning. But that is a myth for another day.

MINDFUL MOMENT FOR WELLBEING: BLUE SKIES

For many centuries, Buddhists have believed that the path to enlightenment can be found through meditation. Their belief is that many of the troubles in the world are caused by looking at the world through the wrong lens.

Whether you are a follower of the Buddhist religion or not, the benefits of meditation are irrefutable. Meditation can help us to slow down and disconnect from our modern-day lives and any damaging habits we may have. It can help to reduce stress, control anxiety and have an overall calming effect. In some ways, stories allow us to do this. Certainly, listening to a story can be a mindful activity if you absorb yourself in the narrative.

The following script will guide you through a mindful moment for wellbeing in which we explore the blue sky above us and the many deities said to reside there. If you have a sunny day with a clear sky for this exercise, all the better as the colour blue can help to relax us, lowering blood pressure and heart rate. Below is a scripted version of this meditation but you can find an audio version via the website page associated with this book. You can find the website link in the introduction.

Before we begin you may want to gather the following things together:

A drink – hot or cold
A blanket to lie on
A warm jumper or spare blanket in case you get cold
Sunglasses if it's sunny

Blue-Sky Meditation

If you would like a cold or hot drink, make one before you start, then find a comfortable place outside to lie or sit, preferably somewhere soft like the grass or on a blanket, where you are warm and safe and it is quiet. You might want to take an extra blanket or jumper, even if it's a warm day, as the body naturally cools as you relax. If it's a sunny day, you might want to wear sunglasses and, remember, never look directly at the sun.

Settle yourself where you have chosen to sit or lie and let your mind relax. Forget the toing and froing of the day, forget the lists, the to-dos and the dones; we are going to focus on the sky.

Close your eyes. Feel your breath moving throughout your body. Feel it move from your head to your toes and back. Feel it ebb and flow along the length of your spine.

Bring your attention to your arms: relax and feel them sink into the earth. Let the earth hold you.

Focus on each part of your arms as you do this.

First your left arm: shoulder ... biceps ... elbow ... forearm ... wrist ... hand ... fingers ... thumb ... index ... middle ... ring ... little finger.

Feel your breath flow through your muscles.

Next do the same with your right arm: shoulder ... biceps ... elbow ... forearm ... wrist ... hand ... fingers ... thumb ... index ... middle ... ring ... little finger.

Feel your breath flow through your muscles.

Feel your breath moving throughout your body.

Feel it move from your head to your toes and back.

Feel it ebb and flow along the length of your spine.

Follow the breath along your spine, relaxing the muscles of your chest and your stomach.

Turn your focus to your legs: allow them to relax and begin to sink into the cool earth.

First your left leg ... your hip ... your thigh ... your knee ... your shin ... your ankle ... your foot ... into your toes.

Then the right leg... your hip ... your thigh ... your knee ... your shin ... your ankle ... your foot ... into your toes.

When you are completely relaxed, slowly open your eyes and look up into the sky. Remember, do not look directly at the sun.

Watch the short waves of light scatter easily.

Celestes ... azures and cyans ... cobalts ... sapphires and cornflowers.

Look closely at the blues: watch them swirl together, watch them dance and drift, a magical paint palate in the sky.

If there are clouds there, notice them.

Delicate cirrus, swirling paintbrush flicks of white, threading in and out of the light; contrails and ice crystals, they streak across the blue canvas.

Closer, cumulus gather their familiar cottonwool shape, lit by the rays of the sun. Beside them floats a soft dove-grey duvet of nimbus.

The closest of all is stratus. It hides the light from us, greying the sky.

Cirrus, cumulus, nimbus and stratus, let them all float by. As the sun completes its arc each day, it will guide you and bring you out into the blue skies.

Imagine the sky surrounding you, lifting you, holding you as the earth does.

You are entering the portal to the gods, blue as Athena the huntress's eyes, the road of the hirundines; swifts, swallows and martins. Each year they follow the sun and trust zephyrs to hold them. Float up to meet them.

Look into the sky and watch the short waves of light scatter easily.

Celestes … azures and cyans … cobalts … sapphires and cornflowers.

Push back the clouds and enter the land of the celestial beings.

The ancient ones.

Hear their stories and walk among them.

First there was Hausos. Soon others followed her into the sky.

From Greece, Helios arrives in a chariot, all-seeing, his shining crown the sun, and Eos, goddess of the dawn, opens the gates for the peach-coloured sunrise to spread across the land, all the while listening for the song of her lost lover.

The Celts bring Lugh, the shining one, and from Rome comes Aurora, who announces the sun's arrival each day. Sol of the north now pulls her chariot beside Helios across the sky, the sun sitting tight within it, Sköll the wolf ever closer behind.

As the world turns towards the sun, from Africa comes Aten,

Dazbog from the Slavic lands,

Shams from Arabia,

Horus from Egypt,

from India comes Surya,

China's Taiyang Xingjun,

Amaterasu of Japan

and Bila from Australia.

They all hold the sun and guide it through the sky. Watch them as they rise.

Thousands of years of myth, legend and story, they are all there, shining through.

Celestes … azures and cyans … cobalts … sapphires and cornflowers.

Stay here and dance with them a while. Follow them as they move across the sky, bask in the warmth they hold, sing to them and let your soul meet theirs.

The dance is done for today and the sun is moving onwards and away. It is time for us to leave the deities of the sky in their endless task. It is time for us to trust that they will bring the sun around again. It is time for us to ask them once more to guide us as they do the sun.

Slowly close your eyes and focus once more on your breathing.

Notice the movement in your chest and stomach as you breath in and out.

Take three deep breaths, pushing the breath down into your feet, up through your spine and out through your head.

When you feel ready, start to gentle rotate your ankles a few times.

Then bend your knees ...

Rotate your wrists and gently move your arms ...

Open your eyes.

If you are not already sitting, push down through the ground with the palms of your hands to slowly sit up.

You have completed your journey to the blue skies and beyond. Take a moment to re-centre, have a sip of your drink and feel the warmth of the sun on your face.

SEPTEMBER

LIFE-GIVER

OUR VILLAGE IS IN A valley with the main street running east to west. As I have headed towards the sunrise each month, I have walked along the street, taken the footpath that climbs the west slope and sat with my back to the tree-line, facing east to watch the sun make its appearance. This evening I have decided to follow the footpath up the downs on the east slope, so that I may sit facing west for the sunset.

This project started with a desire to greet the sun and connect with it as the earth turned towards its life source, but I am now called to watch it disappear. Perhaps the shorter days of autumn are beckoning me into the dark, or the shift in the seasons has me chasing the light. Either way, here I am ascending the fields to sit above the village and watch our largest star disappear for the night.

Many of the fields I walk through are farmed. Blood, sweat and tears have been poured into the land so that it may provide us with sustenance. This farm is undergoing a complete change by moving to organic methods of farming – a lengthy process that takes place over five years. They have created nature corridors and field margins, which encourage pollinators. They have planted crops to restore the balance in the soil, which has long been drained of its vital components, and a little way away, across the fields, there is a bench made from the wood of a tree that fell victim to the storms earlier this year.

For millennia we have relied on the earth for food and resources, in one form or another, and for at least the last 5,000 years we have been managing the land for human convenience.

Initially we worked with the land, paying attention to the seasons, where the sun was and when the rains came. The world wars, almost eighty years ago now, saw not only a need for homegrown food in order to secure supply for the nation, but also a huge leap in the technology that allowed us to do this. The drive towards more efficient farming techniques ultimately led to the monocultures we have today, and methods using pesticides and chemicals that work against nature.

The South Downs National Park that I am walking through is unique in that it is a living, working landscape. Over 75 per cent of the National Park is farmed or worked in some way. Through the 'Farming in Protected Landscapes' scheme facilitated by the Department for Environment, Food and Rural Affairs, farmers can receive funding for projects that mitigate climate change, support communities and nature recovery, and promote land access for visitors.

With schemes such as this one there is a burgeoning movement turning away from monocultures, recognising that whilst this type of farming produces quantity, it is not sustainable and does not always produce quality. If only for our own sakes, we need to start working with nature again rather than against it.

Of course, I have simplified the situation greatly and the farming conundrum is multifaceted and complex. We need food and, at the last count, there were just over 67 million of us in the UK that needed feeding, but there is at least some hope, in the form of these projects, that we can find a more sustainable way to do this.

This summer's drought, coupled with irrigation issues, means that farmers have found it excruciatingly hard to produce quality food to feed the population. The sun giveth and the sun taketh away.

As I walk up through the fields on the east side of the village, I can see clearly how the crops on the steep downland slope catch every last ray of the sun as it arcs across the sky and down behind the hills on the other side of the valley, leaving brush strokes of pink as it goes. As I walk, I am reminded of the weather lore and sayings of past farmers:

> Red sky at night, shepherd's delight,
> Red sky in the morning, shepherd's warning.

I wonder what the sky will bring in this evening's sunset?

At the beginning of the month, we crossed the threshold of meteorological autumn. Around 95 per cent of UK crops have been harvested. The fields lie in stubble and scattered beans, and the ground-nesting birds have long since flown their nests.

Down in the village someone is celebrating and the dulcet tones of a covers band drift up through the cool evening air: Oasis, Elvis, The Eagles, even Prince's 'Purple Rain'. On this side of the village there are a series of meadows and fields. The meadows are grazed by sheep and in between the patchwork of squares, rectangles and triangles are a series of gates, which need to be kept shut to protect the livestock. A chattering family of long-tailed tits gather in the brambles and elder to my left as I walk through the small patches of trees and scrub that mark the boundaries of each field.

To my right, at the furthest edge of the field, there is a well-established bonfire and the smoke drifts lazily along the valley, tracking back east to west. It has been a long, hot summer and this kind of bonfire could not even have been considered three weeks ago. The land was parched and dry, a tinderbox waiting for a spark. Thankfully, the thunderstorms of the last fortnight have greened the landscape once more and the bonfire is not likely to be a problem if well attended. As I ascend the hill, the sun is low and appears hazy through the smoke; the light catches wisps of vapour as they drift lazily along the edge of the field.

When smoke descends, good weather ends.

I reach the top of the hill and the spot I have chosen to sit in. Behind me is a narrow strip of trees and an understorey comprised of wild rose, clematis, brambles and ground elder. The result of the drought is a contrary plethora of plump ripe blackberries on all the brambles I have encountered this year. My daughter and I have already stained our thumbs, fingers and lips with them on late afternoon walks. They are sweeter than any year I remember and I wonder at the hope of nature. Even when it finds itself dying from a lack of water, instead of rolling over, it funnels all its energy into the next generation.

I take up my position for the sunset vigil and from this spot I can see aircraft trails cutting across perfect Turneresque cumulus clouds, tinted lilac and subtle pinks, above a sea of trees on the east ridge where I usually sit. The sun wears a thick halo.

A ring around the sun or moon means rain or snow is coming soon.

It is too bright to look to the horizon for long, so I turn and examine more closely the tree line behind me and discover who my neighbours will be for the next hour or so. These are the trees that I usually watch the sun come up over, where the rooks dance and the birds chatter.

The sight of an ash tree warms my soul; once common in the UK, thanks to ash dieback this is fast becoming a rare resident of our woodlands. Its leaves are almost translucent against the bright blue of the sky.

In Ireland the ash is part of a trilogy of sacred trees: oak, ash and hawthorn. On Creevna Island there stood a sacred ash tree and it is said that there are still descendants of this tree living today. In the nineteenth century, twigs from the descendants of the Creevna tree were carried by emigrants to the USA as a means of protection against drowning on the long journey to their new home.

We still have some ancient ash trees in the UK. Glen Lyon, in Scotland, is home to the oldest ash tree of its kind. Its diameter measures 6½m and it is estimated to be between 300 and 400 years old.

In the grounds of Gordon Castle in Morayshire there is a truly impressive ash with a trunk diameter of almost 9m. This tree is thought to have been planted around 1769.

In many cases pollarding could be the reason for the longevity of these trees. In Bradfield woods, in Suffolk, there is the stump of a coppiced ash tree known as a stool that is 5½m in diameter and thought to be potentially 1,000 years old.

In the seventeenth century, the famous botanist Nicholas Culpeper recommended eating ash seeds because 'the kernels within the husks commonly called ashen keys … prevaileth against stitches and pains in the side'. As ash trees are in the olive tree family, the keys are quite tasty when green, fresh and pickled, and they are thought to cure many stomach ailments.

The tree was also thought to cure many other ills, such as warts and birth defects. In some villages a hole would be made in the ash tree and a shrew placed into it. The ash would then grow over the hole and the village would have itself a magical tree, perfect for healing. Not so perfect for the shrew.

There are many place names in the UK that hold the name of the ash – Ashurst, Ashcombe, Ashbourne, Ashbrittle, Ashley, Ashwell, Ashford, Askrigg, Ashdown Forest, Ashby, Ashill, Ashingdon – in fact according to the *Oxford Dictionary of British Place Names* there are over forty different places in the UK with ash in the name.

This ash, from where I stand at least, is healthy and strong, and I feel honoured indeed to sit beneath a tree that holds so much history and life within it.

A rustling in the trees behind me breaks through my thoughts, and as I search the scrub for the source of the noise, I notice bronzing burgundy dock that grows amongst grumpy old nettles, more medicine within the hedgerows.

I am sitting between a man-made food source and nature's bounty, and here, both have the advantage of soaking up the late afternoon sun.

Folklore that we now remember as being quaint and curious is in fact what would have guided the hedge witches and haywards of the past, those who held the knowledge of the hedgerows. We can, of course, still harness this ancient wisdom with the added benefit of books and science to help us avoid any mishaps.

It is warm where I am sitting in the glow of the sun's last rays, but as soon as a cloud drifts in front of the sun the cooler air of the September evening creeps in. Rooks in the tree line behind me shout at each other that it is time for bed. A long line of stratus cloud drifts over the sun in parallel with the trail of bonfire smoke that drifts its way along the valley. Crochets of birds fly home to roost and a thin strip of orange starts to build below the clouds.

In the opposite direction there are perfect lines across the undulating fields left by the combines and tractors. As the sun dips, it starts to get cooler still and I am glad I brought a hot drink with me – this time lemon balm tea rather than the caffeine-infused coffee that the morning sunrises require.

Fresh lemon balm and mint teas are my favourite for an evening beverage, not least because they are so easy to grow as herbs in the garden, soaking up the sun's goodness and infusing the tea with its light.

The orange evening light deepens. With ten minutes to go before the official Met Office sunset, the sun starts to drop quickly, a bright burning above the trees. Car drivers have already begun putting their headlights on, or at least the auto-sensors on the windshield have decided they should.

A fly's wings iridesce as it rests on a blade of grass, house martins literally fly south and brushstrokes of pink and orange spread across the horizon, all the colours of the day bleeding into the earth.

The sun is now behind the trees; a bright glow of embers and the smoke from the bonfire hangs in an inverted cloud around 3m above the ground. Dark deep-blue night creeps in.

A couple of partygoers from down in the village wander up the hill on their way back to their bed and breakfast. A woman and a man. The woman expresses a concern for me being out in the countryside at this time of night. 'It will be dark soon,' she says. 'You take care.' I thank her and assure her that I know this place.

A tawny owl hoots and with the sun almost completely disappeared it will indeed be dark soon. I pack up my things and begin my descent from the down. As I do, I can hear the revellers in the valley sing 'Happy Birthday' and there are tiny squares of light from the windows of houses that echo the sun that has now set.

In the meadow, the church bells strike eight o'clock and, as if on cue, the bats join me, flitting to and from the trees, following the same diagonal line as the path. They fly not more than 30cm above my head and, in the twilight, I can see that they are catching tiny, translucent white micro moths. Without a bat detector I cannot be sure what they are, but the height, the way they fly and their size (about the same size as a robin) suggests they are probably pipistrelle bats.

A full moon and a clear night give me enough light for the walk home and under the trees there are the grey shapes of grazing sheep in the meadow who barely look up. They can most definitely see better than me in the ever increasing dark and seem unperturbed by my presence.

In the gloaming the bush crickets sing in the scrub and long grass. With the last of the sun's warmth still deep in my bones, it almost feels Mediterranean. Like the bats, crickets are crepuscular and plentiful in the downland in which I live. Bush crickets are easy to spot and are, as their name suggests, dark brown.

Crickets are thought to be lucky and in some cultures are a symbol of wealth. In Ireland, the cricket's singing is thought to keep away the fairies, and I take comfort in this as I walk along the path, confident that I will not be spirited away on my way home through the half-light. In Greek myth, crickets or cicadas represent a lost love and I am reminded of the story of a mortal and a sun goddess. It is this story that I would like to tell you.

EOS AND TITHONUS

Below is my retelling of the stories that surround the Greek goddess of the sun, Eos. As often with Greek myths, there are many different versions and I have read through several of them and used several different sources, including encyclopaedias that detail the Greek pantheon, in order to craft my own.

Let me tell you of Eos and Tithonus. Eos is a Titaness. She's not just a goddess, she's one of the first of the nature goddesses. She lives in a palace in Oceanus and each morning with her saffron and gold robes she pushes the sun up into the sky with her rosy fingers. She is the daughter of Hyperion, bringer of light, and Thea the divine. She is sister to Helios and Selene, the sun and the moon, and her job is to open the mighty sky gates and allow the dawn to spread out into the earth, pushing the veil of Nix back beneath the rocks and into the caves and dark places. Eos is a glorious being.

However, Eos has a burden. You see there was a time when Eos loved Aries; beautiful Aries, the god of war. Those days were joyous days, full of love and light for Eos, but Aries belonged to Aphrodite and, well, Hades has nothing on a goddess scorned. So, when Aphrodite found out, which of course was inevitable, she took her vengeance on Eos. Not Aries, oh no, she loved Aries despite his affair; she took her vengeance on Eos. Aphrodite cursed Eos, proclaiming that from that day forth Eos would only ever love mortal men and that her love would never be returned.

Eos didn't see this as too much of a problem for a Titaness such as herself, until she discovered that what she also had was an insatiable lust for the earth-bound humans.

The first to fall foul of this was Orion. Now in some stories you will read that Orion was never going to love any woman, but in others you will find that he did indeed love a goddess but that it was not Eos. It was, of course, Artemis, for Orion was a great hunter, making him and Artemis the perfect love match. They would hunt together for days on end. When Eos tried to take Orion away from Artemis, this ended very badly in a sibling rift between Artemis and Apollo, but that is a story for another day. It is not Eos' story. But let's just say Orion now lives in the sky.

Next was Cephalus. Cephalus was a handsome youth, just married. When Eos looked down upon him, she fell so in lust that she could not help herself and abducted him. Things went well for a while and, despite Cephalus's situation, he and Eos had three children together. But Cephalus missed his mortal wife and he complained of this to Eos, who told him that his wife would not have waited for him or been faithful as humans never were. But Cephalus would not believe her and wanted desperately to return to his wife. Eos set him a test. She disguised him in order to see if his wife remained faithful. Cephalus returned to earth and visited his wife, seducing her in his disguise and thus discovering that she had indeed not been faithful, and so it was that that affair did not end well either.

Finally, there was Tithonus, a prince of Troy. He again was very handsome and when Eos turned her face upon him and called to him, he looked up at her and for the first time a mortal fell in love with Eos. She could not have been more joyful at the discovery that he returned her love. Their life was to be a very happy one.

They lived for many years in Eos' palace in Oceanus, Eos taking the sun across the sky with her chariot led by her horses Firebright and Daybright. They raised three children and their life too was full of light and love.

But Tithonus, as handsome as he was and as in love with Eos as he was, was still mortal and he started to age. The lines of the joy and happiness they had experienced etched themselves on his face and his hair turned the colour of moonlight. Eos could see that Tithonus could not stay with her for the entirety of her life and so she came up with a plan.

Meanwhile, Aphrodite had been watching Eos and Tithonus and it burnt her up inside. She could not allow this to happen; Eos was supposed to be cursed, she was never meant to be this happy and yet here she was, living blissfully with a mortal.

When Eos took her plan to Zeus, there standing behind him, with a smile creeping into the corners of her mouth, was Aphrodite.

Zeus looked down at Eos and said, 'I hear you have come to me about a mortal.'

'I have, Zeus. I love him and so I have come to beg of you to give him immortality.'

'I have been speaking to Aphrodite here and she sees that you two are very much in love. She is of the opinion that I should grant you this wish.'

Eos could not believe what she was hearing. Aphrodite was going to allow this to happen. Perhaps the goddess of love had softened.

'I will give you what you want,' said Zeus, 'and I will grant Tithonus immortality.'

Well, Eos could not believe it. She ran all the way back to Tithonus and gave him the news. The children rejoiced that their father would be with them for ever, in the golden palace on the edge of the horizon.

Their days would be long and happy.

Indeed, the days did roll on and soon became years, and Eos noticed that Tithonus was still ageing. The lines on his face became deeper, his bones were sharp under his stretched and sagging skin, and his hair thinned and frayed. His eyes started to cloud and his bones began to ache. She could not understand how, if Zeus had granted her request, this could be happening.

A hundred years or more passed and Tithonus could hardly move. He would lie all day on his bed, a bag of bones. He strained to speak but eventually, no matter how hard he tried, there was no sound that came from his broken vocal cords.

Eos had no choice but to return to Zeus and ask what had happened.

And so, she returned to the great god Zeus, and there behind Zeus stood Aphrodite who was now laughing.

Zeus looked at Eos. 'Eos, Titaness of the dawn, you did not ask me for eternal youth, you only asked me for immortality. Tithonus will never die, but that does not mean he will not age.'

Eos was bereft. There was nothing she could do, for the gods cannot retract their blessings, even if they turn out to be a curse, and Aphrodite had no intention of lifting her curse from Eos – in fact, she had just made it worse.

Eos returned to her husband and her boys and she looked at Tithonus. She did not know what to do. Tithonus, had he been able to, would have begged to die. Every inch of him ached and his senses were barely in existence.

Eos decided that she would do the one thing that she could do for Tithonus and she turned her beautiful, loving husband into a cricket.

Now, you may ask, why create such a tiny creature from such a mighty man? Well, that little cricket sits in the meadows and still sings to Eos as she disappears each day below the horizon, taking the sun with her. And so, it is as Shakespeare once said: 'If music be the food of love, play on.' Well then, Tithonus, as a little cricket, still plays music to Eos, the goddess of the dawn.

PICKLES, PRESERVES AND CHUTNEYS

For me this story reminds us of the fleeting nature of abundance and that nothing can last for ever.

Each year in the late summer and in autumn we reap the rewards of the hard work of many farmers across the land, and indeed the world, in the form of vegetables and fruit.

These days we have access to this abundance all year round, but there was a time when everyone grew their own food and had to make the produce of summer and autumn harvests last as long as possible. They did this through curing meats, smoking fish and pickling and preserving fruit and vegetables. Below are three of my favourite recipes for prolonging the abundance of the harvest.

As you are following these recipes, you might take a moment to think about the warmth of the sun and the role it has played in bringing the harvest to our kitchens.

Pickled Leeks

I love pickled onions. Pickled leeks, also in the Allium family, are a close second. This is a very simple recipe that uses short leeks. These are the first leeks to be harvested in the early mid-summer and are usually a bit smaller than autumn leeks. If you miss the short/early leeks at the beginning of the season, you can use leeks later in the season but they are not quite as sweet. Either way, pickled leeks are delicious with mid-winter cheese and crackers.

Ingredients

4 short leeks
320ml of cider vinegar
20ml of water
3 sprigs of fresh chervil, rosemary or a herb of your choice
3 bay leaves
Zest and juice of one lemon
1tsp of table salt
2tsp of yellow mustard seeds
A 600ml sterilised jar (see notes below)

Method

- Slice the leeks thinly and wash them thoroughly to get rid of any soil or grit from the fields, then put them to one side.
- Add all the ingredients, except the leeks, to a large pan.
- Bring the liquid to the boil and simmer for two minutes.
- Put the washed, sliced leeks into the sterilised jar.
- Remove the liquid from the heat and cool completely.
- Once the liquid has cooled, pour it over the leeks in the jar, ensuring they are completely covered by the liquid.
- Label the jar, refrigerate and eat within two weeks.

Orange Chutney

Delicious festive fare that uses the glut of small oranges we have at this time of year. It's another great winter cheese-board accompaniment.

Ingredients

3 small oranges: clementine, tacle or satsuma
3 shallots, finely chopped
2 medium Bramley apples, peeled and roughly chopped
200g of demerara sugar
200ml of cider vinegar
1tsp of yellow mustard seeds
1 fresh bay leaf
1 small cinnamon stick
600g sterilised jar (see notes below)

Method

- Grate or zest oranges, leaving the white pith behind on the orange.
- Place the zest of the orange in a medium saucepan that will eventually hold all of the ingredients.
- Cut away the remaining white pith from the oranges, discard the pith and dice up the flesh.
- Add the orange to the saucepan with all the other ingredients.
- Place over the heat, bring to the boil and then simmer on a low heat until it is thickened and reduced to a chutney-like consistency.
- Stir regularly to prevent the moisture from sticking to the bottom of your pan.

- You can check it's ready by placing a small amount on a cold plate. As it cools, a film should form on top of the mixture on the plate.
- When it's ready, remove the bay leaves and cinnamon stick and pour into the warm, sterilised jar.
- Cover tightly with lids, allow to cool and label the jar.
- Store in a cool, dark place and use within one month.

Apple Butter

I make this spread almost every year with the apples from our tree. Best served on toast like a jam, it's a great recipe for using up windfall.

Ingredients

1.5kg of windfall apples
500ml of cider
Sugar (see below)
½tsp ground cloves
½tsp ground cinnamon
Enough jars to hold 1kg of apple butter

Method

- Wash the apples and then cut them into chunks, getting rid of any bruised bits on the compost heap.
- Place the apples in a large, heavy-bottomed pan with the cider and another 500ml of water.
- Bring to the boil and then lower to a simmer until the fruit is soft.
- Once cooled, sieve into a large bowl and clean out the fruit pan.

- Weigh out the pulp and put it back into the cleaned pan.
- Simmer until the fruit thickens.
- To calculate how much sugar you will need, work out three quarters of the fruit's weight from the measurement you took earlier and add the sugar to the fruit. For example, if you have used 600g of fruit, you will need 450g of sugar.
- Now add the spices.
- Gently heat whilst stirring to ensure all the sugar is dissolved. Keep the fruit mixture on a low heat until there is no free-running liquid. You can test for this by placing a small drop on a plate and seeing if water pools around it. If it doesn't, keep going until it does.
- Finally, pour into sterilised jars and label.
- How to sterilise jam jars: wash the jars with warm water and then place them (without the lid) on an oven tray in the oven at 110°C for 15 minutes. Ensure the jars are cooled before filling them.
- You can download labels for your jars of pickles, chutney and jam via the website page for this book. You will find the web address in the introduction.

OCTOBER

ADJUSTING TO THE DARK

IT'S PITCH BLACK AND THE owls are calling, as I turn the key in the front door to lock it behind me. I look up at the sky in time to see a shooting star. It's 6.30 a.m. when I leave the house and it's a clear cloudless sky. I can see the constellations of Ursa Major, Ursa Minor and Orion clearly. Blinking beside them are early morning planes with their port and starboard lights.

As I walk, once more, along the main street through the village, there many more signs of human life compared to the unsociable hours of summer sunrises. The lights are on in the village shop and Chris, who delivers the papers, is loading up his car.

There is a fingernail moon in its waxing crescent phase and I can see the sky changing colour as I walk, but for now we are still in astronomical twilight. It's almost the end of October and I've busted out the interim fleece trousers, but as I walk, I find it's actually quite a mild 13°C and I am thoroughly overdressed, again.

It's a week before the clocks go back and we reclaim some of the light. Unsympathetic headlights on the cars of early Saturday workers night-blind me on the footpath. My ears hear the puddles beneath my feet, gutters spatter with overflow and gullies sing with last night's rain.

Many crepuscular creatures have a *tapetum lucidum*, a thin reflective surface just behind their retina. This helps them to see more clearly in the dark. Humans lack this helpful addition. Beneath the tree-lined path, in this light, I am a clumsy animal and the undergrowth, nourished by days of rain, meets in front of me in a tangle of unseen ivy and bramble that reaches down to brush against my face, as the nettles stretch up and cling to my fingers. I relent and search in my pocket for a torch. In its grey glow the tree branches are finger-like.

The torch creates a Blair Witch-style circle. I've never been good at horror or psychological thrillers; some would say my imagination is far too vivid to be able to leave behind the terror invoked by a film I have just watched. That 1999 film stayed with me for a long time. Now, over twenty years later, those irrational emotions well up in me once more.

I long to get up into the field to the known turf and expanse of meadow in which I can see clearly. Despite the many mornings I have climbed this hill, I still do not know every dip and tree root of the path and I am nervous, as the veil thins and we enter the liminal space between night and day.

It doesn't take long before I realise I forgot to check the torch was charged and it gives up on me halfway up the corridor of undergrowth. But instead of the half-light consuming me, it seems to hold me safe once more.

The tawny owls are calling to each other again and I am reassured further by the k'wik of a female tawny owl behind me in the woods. I note that we have almost come full circle with the days from the reign of the songbird to the eve of the owl.

I stuff my coat into my backpack. It's clear I do not need the layers that I am wearing, given the mild weather and the pace at which my brain has insisted I walk in order to avoid the dark unknown. Above the field the stars are starting to fade but the sliver of moon is still bright.

With the arrival of a new contract, I have been office based for the last three months and so I have had to adjust to not being able to go for my usual random walks when I feel like it. As a result, the dwindling evening sun and the electric lights have left me feeling tired and lethargic, no matter how much sleep I get.

Seasonal adjustment disorder (SAD) and the benefits of natural light are well documented and daylight lamps are readily available to buy, promising the healing power of the sun. For me, there is no comparison to breathing in the fresh air and feeling the sun on your face. I sit in the too-wet-to-be-sat-in grass, taking up my usual spot, and I wait for the light to return, warm my bones and calm my mind.

It is the sun's ultraviolet B, more commonly referred to as UVB rays, that allows us to create vitamin D within our skin. Studies show that there are few days during the winter months in the UK that the sun is high enough and strong enough to deliver the amount of UVB that the average human body requires in order to produce adequate vitamin D. At this time of year, we must therefore rely on our diets to do this. Milk, oily fish, egg yolks and red meat are the best sources of this vitamin, vital for bone and muscle health. A ready supply of vitamin supplements on supermarket and health-food shop shelves also helps. Heliophiles travel abroad at this time of year, and who can blame them when every part of your body craves the dwindling light?

There are records showing that, as far back as 3,500 years ago, we humans recognised the role of the sun and the light it emits in our overall health. The Egyptian Ebers Papyrus, a document thought to have been recorded in 1550 BCE, talks of sun worship as a cure for certain medical complaints. Perhaps that is the first mention of photodynamic therapy, which today is used to treat dermatological conditions and some skin cancers. Other elements of the sun's spectrum, such as green light, has been found to help with chronic pain.

We need the sun. We know that, it's instinctual, yet our lives have somehow often become optimised for working in dark little boxes away from the natural world.

It's good to feel the ground beneath me, earthing my excess nervous energy.

I have a full week of storytelling events ahead of me for the October half term and I seek the earth to steady me as I move the once-familiar stories I will be telling to the front of my brain and cement the new ones I will be recounting this year. A car alarm sounds as the clock on the church strikes seven o'clock.

The woods begin to wake and I can hear a wren, buzzard and pheasant. A thin layer of mist creeps up the hill as the moisture condenses and the ground temperature slowly rises. A pheasant bursts out of the treeline. It's a peculiar sight as it's not at the height you'd expect and lands in a tree 6 or 7m off the ground.

The animals seem anxious this morning. There is more arguing in the trees behind me, the winter resident birds marking their territories perhaps, knowing that this is more crucial than ever as the winter will soon be here and supplies must be secured.

A line of dove-grey cloud mirrors the tree line on the far ridge, a ridge I am very familiar with now. This ridge, in my mind, is forever the one where rooks hop along the tree tops gathering their fellows before flying out at sunup to find new foraging grounds. Thirty minutes to sunrise and the rooks get noisy, waking up for the day. They leapfrog along the distant tree-lined ridge, gathering more comrades as they go. A chaotic toing and froing, not the balletic murmuration starlings will treat you to.

A switch is flicked and bright pink strips herald the sun; the occasional runner and dog walker start to appear. Sheep huddle in the still-cold fields of the downs and the owls' calls have given way to the urgent calling of a firecrest.

Horizontal shards of yellow light spill out from the brilliant blue sky scattered with underlit clouds. The sun is up but there's still a chill in the air. With a mental list of things to do today, my time is up and I pack up my coffee and head down the hill. As I walk back through the woods, the squirrels squawk at each other and the toes of my boots are covered in wet grass clippings.

The sun continues rising gradually and the light finds me through the trees. It feels as if I have emerged from a dark and dingy crepuscular world into a bright sunlit Eden, and again I am reminded that we have come full circle as my thoughts echo those I had in March when this walk back felt like I was emerging from a fairy world.

As we have seen in previous chapters, there are many underworlds and otherworlds contained in story, from myth to urban legend, and portals to other worlds are frequently accompanied by a change in light – the feeling of stepping into the light from a world where you were once lost, whether that be a new world or one you are familiar with. The story that accompanies this chapter is an urban legend from the Middle Ages that is still told today. It is a story of stepping from the dark into the light.

GREEN CHILDREN O' WOOLPIT

Wol'pit or Woolpit, as it later became known, is the name of a village in Suffolk, England, that is thought to have been called this because of the deep pits dug on the outer edges of the village to protect the livestock from wolves, known as wolf pits. The sign for Woolpit village, with its depiction of two children, is a nod to this story and this is my interpretation of a local legend that is over 900 years old.

The church bells were still ringing out as the two strangers walked across the meadows, hunched and squinting at the sun. I was late back from worship and walking across fields of stubble when I saw them. Lost they were. The words they spoke were not those of our country. Their skin was tinged with green and their pupils were pin-pricks with the light. Their faces gaunt with worry and hunger, I hurried them home to the little cottage where my husband and I live with our own children, all five of them usually working in the fields, but that day, Sunday, they were home.

They were busy putting out the bread and butter for our mid-morning vittles, filling up the kettle over the fire and laughing about how the vicar had said this or that, that morning in the sermon, and how red in the face he went when one of the other wee children had squawked in the middle of his profound words.

They fell silent when I came in with the green children, before crowding around to ask who they were and where they came from.

I shushed them and told them to bring the children some food, but the strangers refused all the food offered. Bread, ham, apples, cheese, nothing seemed to please them until I realised their gaze was fixed on the broad beans.

That year there had been a plentiful crop of broad beans and one end of my kitchen table was covered in them, where I was salting and preserving them for the dark days of winter. I took a couple of the full pods and offered them. They took 'em quick as you like and devoured them. It's all they ate for the next month.

I knew I'd have to speak to the village council sooner rather than later, and that evening, whilst the children I'd found out by the wol'pits slept in the same beds as my own children, I called the elders together.

I told them all I knew of them. That they had come from the direction of the wol'pits on the edge of the village and no one, not no one, knew who they were.

I thought perhaps they might be Flemish and I feared for their lives as our king was much aggrieved with those from Flanders fleeing famine to find a home on these isles. I thought perhaps their parents had been victims of his harsh policy and begged the rest of the village to keep them safe and quiet here.

They agreed but it wasn't long before the lord of the manor, up the way, took a fancy to the young girl. She had wild ways that appealed to him and so he offered her employ. The brother went with her too, but he didn't last. He was frail and the work was too much. He died just under a year after I found him that day walking across the meadow. Pneumonia.

She, the girl that is, went on to marry the lord. Lived a good life, learnt our language and, I'm pleased to say, ate more than broad beans eventually. That said, the Lord would still pay a good penny to anyone providing the sweetest broad beans that summer for his beloved wol'pit girl.

In later years, once she could speak our words, she would often gather the children in the village square and tell them of how she and her brother had come from an otherworld, a fairy-world, under the ground, where there was no light and everything was green. She told them that on that day when I'd found them, they had journeyed through the tunnels and, walking out into the sunlight, they had become blinded and disorientated. They had followed the ringing of the bells from the church towards the village and that's when I'd found them.

Of course, there was gossip that this was not the case at all. Whilst we all believed in the good folk of the land, we knew them to be illusive and tricksy, not at all like these children had been.

The local doctor muttered that they must have been victims of some sort of plague or ailment, and that they had been given a tincture of arsenic to try and cure them. It is known that this can leave a green tinge to the skin. Perhaps the plague had taken their parents and the children were left to roam as orphans until I found them?

I was just happy I had been able to offer them shelter and that at least the girl had survived and done well for herself. If she was Flemish, as I thought they must have been, her story of her otherworld kept her safe in many ways and allowed her to dance in the sun without fear of the authorities. I'm glad of that and so are those in the pub this night who, I have no doubt, still tell this tale and will do for many more years to come.

JOURNALLING IN THE DARK DAYS

Nature journalling has become a popular pastime amongst all ages. As the days grow shorter, now is the perfect time to slow down and take a moment to notice the toing and froing of your local flora and fauna. There may be less of it, but that makes it easier to spot. It also gets you out for some vital natural light.

I have a backpack by the door ready to go for long sits and nature journalling rambles. For nature journalling all you really need is a pencil and a notebook, but here are some of the things I carry with me, which you may find useful:

Propelling pencil with 2B graphite.

A notebook with blank pages – I recommend A5 at least. If you are intending to use watercolours or pens, consider the medium you are using when choosing the paper for your journal.

Coloured pencils.

A decent pencil sharpener that collects the shavings, so you leave no trace if you are outside.

If you want to create a gallery-style nature journal, you might consider having a rough book for notes when you are out and about, and a neat book to create your final pages in.

A backpack, to put it all in.

A sit mat if you are intending to sit for any length of time. You can buy these fairly cheaply or you could make one with a folded newspaper and a plastic bag over the top of it.

Binoculars.

A camera or mobile device with a camera.

A Dictaphone or voice recorder app on your mobile device.

If you are not sure where to start, try just going for a short circular walk without the pressure of a notebook, or sit in the garden with a cuppa. Whilst you are out and about, you may like to ask yourself the following questions:

What do I notice about today?
What is the weather doing?
What feelings does the environment I'm in evoke?
What are my senses telling me?
What can I see in the wider landscape and what can I see up close?

As a curious human being, there are always things you will want to look up later. That's where I find a notebook or Dictaphone come in handy, and something to take photographs with for reference.

Whilst you are out, see if you can find a good spot you can return to and sit for a while to observe the seasons as the wheel of the year turns.

There are many ways to nature journal and there is no right way. I find it a great way of keeping in touch with the seasons and not getting lost in the dark months of winter. Use the link in the introduction to visit the resources page associated with this book, for more information to help you get started.

NOVEMBER

CAPTURING THE LIGHT

AS I HEAD OUT INTO the gloaming, for my first sunrise of November, synthetic light punctuates the silvern twilight. With the sun rising later but the demands of modern life requiring us to rise at the same time as usual, kitchen lights, porch lanterns, fairy lights in bay trees and the clicking on and off of security lights are all more prominent in our village. Even without street lamps there are still plenty of yellow counterfeit suns.

Since the discovery of fire, we have found many ways to capture the light of the sun. The most obvious is electricity. Since its invention we have become reliant on this man-made power to extend our days and create efficient workplaces that allow the maximum productivity possible regardless of the light levels outside.

At this time of year, we have approximately nine hours of light as opposed to around sixteen and a half hours in June. There was a time when our ancestors would have been restricted to completing tasks, in the main, during daylight hours, the light of the fire often proving inadequate for any close work or farming. Electricity thumbs its nose at this and allows us to work twenty-four hours a day should we wish.

It's not just humans that are awake all night though. As previously mentioned, in some urban areas with a good canvas of street lamps, the robins and blackbirds sing all night too. Waders near a power station on the Forth of Firth in Edinburgh are now able to find more food during the night because of the constant low-level light, allowing them to take advantage of once-inaccessible, night-time low tides. The increase in light at night has also been found to disrupt insects and their behaviour. Ultimately, this is one of the reasons for a decline in the number of insects, something that is fast being recognised as having serious consequences for the whole planet.

Skyglow caused by artificial lights increases year on year and LED lights, which promised low-level energy as a solution to increased energy production and a growing carbon footprint, have in fact increased light pollution due to their adaptability and affordability, particularly garden path and fairy lights. This constant light, albeit sometimes at a low level, doesn't just affect the wildlife that lives in our urban sprawl, it affects us. The sun's light triggers our circadian rhythms. It informs our bodies when to raise our blood pressure and heart rate and start to fire the cells in our brains again after sleep. It's literally why we wake up.

I look out across the landscape, from my usual spot, waiting for the sun to rise, and marching across the fields in the middle distance are the pylons of the National Grid. Bringing my focus back to the grass of the meadow, as the sun rises, each blade of grass has a tiny droplet of water on it and just like May's sunrise, each orb is lit by growing light – its own little National Grid.

I am reminded of a little nugget of general knowledge stored in my brain, of lace-makers' lamps. Before electricity was commonplace, lace-makers created lamps that were orbs of glass on stands. The orb was filled with water and stood next to a lit candle. The light from the candle reflected through the orb and created a wider area of light for the lace-maker. If the spiders are lace-makers then these blades of grass and droplets of light are their lamps.

As the days grow shorter and the sun rises later, our reliance on electricity is clear. Electricity may have taken us further away from depending on the sun's light in order to work, but with a greater understanding of climate change and the need for action, we are once more turning to the sun for help.

We have known about solar power since the work of Dr Mária Telkes in 1952 and seventy years on there have been huge advances in photovoltaic technology, with 25 acres of solar panels providing energy for as many as 1,500 homes. Solar power is part of our past, present and future.

I mentioned at the beginning of this chapter that this was the first of my November sunrises, a sunrise where humans' capturing of the light is very evident. For the second sunrise the light was captured in a very different way.

A few months earlier I had been invited to be a part of a photography project run by Dave Tipper, a Hampshire-based photographer. He was exploring how we relate to the landscape by taking a walk with various people from different creative disciplines that were, themselves, connecting with the landscape in different ways. In doing this, he hoped to discover how different people see the landscape and how it influences our practice.

Dave wanted to walk in an area that was familiar to me, so I suggested my sunrise walk. November was agreed upon as the sunrise at this time of year – 7.30 a.m. – isn't entirely antisocial. And so it was that I set off late in November for a second sunrise, this time, and for the first time in this project, with a human companion.

As we walk and talk to the spot where I sit to watch the sunrise, Dave asks me questions for his research. One of the first questions he asks me is why I chose this spot. It is at this point that I am reminded that there were very practical reasons for choosing it. It faces east where the sun will rise, I know where it is and I'm not going to get lost in the gloom of a dark dawn.

It is during this interview that we also discuss how at first I intended to go to different places to watch the sunrise but I have only done this on two occasions: beside the River Tees whilst on holiday and to take in a sunset in September. Instead, I choose to come back to this spot. So, the question is, why do I return here?

I find the answer is that I'm sitting in the middle of the edges, the edges of the village, the edges of the wood and the edges of the field. Flora, fauna and community converge on this spot. I am observing but I too am observed. I am a part, not apart.

As the light changes, our conversation turns to photography. As a photographer Dave notes how, as the light returns, you start to see lots of different pictures as the landscape around you comes into focus. The landscape starts to come to life – in his words, 'Light reveals things, I guess. That's the magic of darkness.'

Dave's project is about belonging and a sense of place. It was a coincidence that we were there for the sunrise, but many people have completed photography projects that specifically involve the sun. One such project is to create an analemma.

As I mentioned in January's chapter, an analemma plots the point at which the sun appears in the sky throughout the year. The sun always rises in the east, but its position is to the north or the south through the year. In January it rises in a north-easterly direction, moving gradually until the solstice in June, when it rises to the south-east and stays in one place for around three days. Then it gradually moves back north. If you take a picture of the sun's position each week for a year and then layer those pictures together, the sun will look like it is moving in a figure of eight or analemma. It's a technically complex project but with fascinating results.

The use of phones for digital photography means that you can easily find pictures of sunrises and sunsets across the world with a quick search of the World Wide Web. Photographic artist Penelope Umbrico collated the most-liked photographs of sunsets from Flickr, an online photo-sharing site. She then put all the pictures together to create an enormous piece of community art – a worldwide sunset.

As Dave and I sit, watching the light change and the sun return, Dave takes photographs for his project and we chat more about the way we connect with the landscape through words and images. We are deep in contemplation of the land when we are interrupted by the local racehorse trainer entering the field.

During the winter the horses train here and we are sitting in the path that they will gallop around. The trainer asks us to move back so that the horses aren't distracted by us. We, of course, oblige and stand on the edge of the wood as the horses thunder around the field, snorting misty breath into the dull light of the new day. Watching them, I am reminded of the three horses that represent the light, from the story of Baba Yaga and Vasilisa.

VASILISA THE BRAVE

This is a very old Russian story famously illustrated by Ivan Bilibin. It was originally passed down through the oral traditions and many people, across the world, are familiar with her. But if you are not, she's a witch that likes to eat people or at least that's what the stories will tell you. For me she is akin to a Cailleach of the land; she is a woman who is wise, has walked many paths and does not suffer fools gladly.

She has a dark side and a light side, and perhaps if you do meet her, if you treat her with respect, she may well turn out to be an ally. For now, I will tell you the story of Vasilisa's meeting with the old crone of the Russian woods.

A long time ago there lived a girl called Vasilisa. She lived with her mother and her father and these were hard times. Although they weren't the poorest of families, Vasilisa's mother had become ill. This had been hard for Vasilisa because she'd had to help around the house and look after the daily management of the smallholding. Her father worked abroad a lot of the time and so looking after her mother also fell to Vasilisa.

Unfortunately, they knew that her mother would pass soon, so Vasilisa's mother called her to her bed and said to her that she knew that she was going and that Vasilisa would be on her own with her father. She said that she hoped that her father would find someone who would keep them both company and look after the house for them. Vasilisa told her not to worry, that she would be able to do it. Her mother handed her a small doll and said, 'Keep this doll close, for it will help you if you ever find yourself in trouble.'

When her mother died that is what Vasilisa did. She kept the doll close. She looked after the doll. She talked to the doll. She sang to the doll. Her father would even, on occasion, find her feeding the doll little bits of food from the table.

In time her father did find somebody and married again. Unfortunately, this woman was not kind to Vasilisa. She had two daughters of her own whom she mothered and she had no wish to mother another daughter. And so it was that Vasilisa was still left with the lion's share of the chores.

She ran the house and looked after her sisters and her stepmother, who were always trying to find favour with their stepfather and show Vasilisa in a bad light. Of course, Vasilisa's father always preferred his daughter and it was difficult for him not to show this. A great hatred grew in the three women, who could never gain the father's attention that Vasilisa had.

Eventually the father went away on exploring on a ship. He promised to bring back riches and wealth from other lands, and while he was gone, the stepmother and the sisters plotted to get rid of Vasilisa.

The stepmother went through the house putting out all of the candles, all of the little oil lamps and all of the fires. There was only one tiny flame left from a candle that stood on the mantelpiece. The stepmother and the daughters steadfastly refused to light the fire again and Vasilisa was home too late after her chores to collect more wood in order to do it. It was dark outside now and not a time to go out looking for wood in the still-darker forest, let alone wood that might be dry enough to burn.

As they sat by the fire sewing, eventually the little candle sputtered out and they began to strain their eyes with the tiny stitches. The stepsisters complained that it was too dark and they would hurt their eyes. They weren't going to go out there and find more wood, Vasilisa would have to do it.

'But we have nothing to light it with,' the stepmother replied. 'Vasilisa will have to go and find fire.'

But Vasilisa was at a loss. 'Where am I going to find fire? There is no one with a hearth for miles around,' she replied.

'You will have to go to Baba Yaga's house.' The three women were in unison.

Now Vasilisa had heard of Baba Yaga. Baba Yaga was not somebody you messed with. Certainly not someone whose door you went up to, knocked on and asked for a candle.

'Yes, that's what she'll have to do,' said the sisters, revelling in the idea. 'She will have to go into the wood and find Baba Yaga's house, and if she cannot come back with fire then she should not come back at all.'

So it was that Vasilisa had no choice: she had to go into the dark woods to find the fire that Baba Yaga held. Through the forest she walked, and as she got closer to the house of Baba Yaga, the wood became quieter and darker, darker and quieter. The trees closed in and the branches reached out, snagging her clothes.

She walked so far that the night became day and as it did a white horse and rider rode through the trees. Next, as the sun appeared on the horizon, a red horse and rider thundered through the pines. Vasilisa walked on for many hours and the woods got quieter and darker, darker and quieter, as the sun disappeared. Soon a black horse and rider burst through the edge of the forest, racing through the middle of it and consuming it in inky blackness.

In the distance Vasilisa saw a faint glow coming from what looked like small windows almost at tree height. As she got closer, she saw that the glow came from a hut that was on chicken legs, high up in the sky, and around it was a fence with skulls on each post, all lit up with a tiny flame.

From trees that surrounded it, an old woman appeared. 'Vasilisa, you have come,' she said.

This must be Baba Yaga, for she had a hooked nose and yellowing craggy teeth, a face lined in a map of her life and no light in her eyes. Yes, this was Baba Yaga.

'I have come for a flame to light our fire. My stepmother has sent me.'

'I know. I know your stepmother and she has sent you to the right place. I will give you fire and you may take it back to your stepmother, but only if you do exactly as I tell you. You will need to do all the chores in the house.'

This was not really a problem for Vasilisa. Not a problem at all. She'd been doing chores for a very long time now and so she went with Baba Yaga into the grounds of the little hut and up the long, winding steps to the door.

On the steps there was a dog that snarled and Baba Yaga told the dog to be still, then a cat that tried to claw Vasilisa and Baba again told the cat to leave Vasilisa alone. Finally, a birch tree growing next to the hut tried to scratch at Vasilisa's face until Baba Yaga said stop. Baba Yaga commanded the door of the hut to open and as it did the hinges creaked and echoed through the forest.

Into the house they went and Baba Yaga showed Vasilisa all of the different chores she would need to do, sweeping, cleaning, washing and cooking, and every day Vasilisa did everything in that house exactly as Baba Yaga asked.

And each day the old woman would sit down and eat a huge feast of boiled, broiled, smoked and roasted meats, and she would not leave a thing for Vasilisa other than the washing up and the bones to clean away.

Eventually Baba Yaga became bored. Bored with the girl who never put a foot wrong. She decided she was going to really test her because Vasilisa was clearly well used to these tasks and completed them with far too much ease. She decided to give her a different sort of task.

'Vasilisa, come here. I have a job for you and if you can complete this task then you can leave with a flame. If you do not then I'll eat you.'

Vasilisa listened, hoping that whatever the task might be, she would be able to complete it.

'Vasilisa, I want you to go into the grain store and sort the grain from the mildew that has settled on it. I want it done by the time the black horse and rider come back through the forest, dragging the veil of night across it.'

Vasilisa was again at a loss; she did not know what to do.

Baba Yaga went out that day in a huge pestle and mortar that she rowed like an enormous, monstrous boat through the trees, and she was gone.

Vasilisa sat down on the cold, hard floor of the chicken-leg hut and sobbed until a tiny voice came from her pocket.

'Why do you cry, Vasilisa?'

Vasilisa wiped the tears from her eyes. She had forgotten that she had left the doll in her pocket, the doll that her mother had given her and that she had kept close ever since her mother had died.

'Hello, little doll,' said Vasilisa, pulling the doll from her pocket. 'You must be hungry – here,' and she took some of the crumbs from the old woman's breakfast off the table and fed them to the little doll. Vasilisa told the doll of all the chores she had to do and how she had to separate the mildew from the grain and that it was surely an impossible task.

The doll said, 'Do not worry, Vasilisa. I will do it for you. You go and rest. Sleep – you look so tired.'

And so Vasilisa, perhaps thinking she was in a dream, did just that, for her mother had told her this doll would look after her and she believed it would.

She woke as she heard the thunder of the dark horse's hooves, and she heard the grinding of the pestle and mortar, and as she did, she discovered all the grain separated out and as clean as the day it had been harvested. Beside it was a tiny pile of mildew. And the little doll? Back in her pocket.

Baba Yaga was furious. There would be no human flesh for her dinner tonight. She would have to find another way to be able to feast on Vasilisa.

'Very good,' she said. 'Very good.' Tomorrow, I have another task for you. I wish for you to sort the dried peas from the poppy seeds, in the store. She took Vasilisa into another little room and showed her an enormous pile of peas and seeds that almost reached the ceiling of the hut.

'Very well,' said Vasilisa for she had little other choice.

'And of course, Vasilisa, I want this done by the time the black horse and rider arrive back through the forest.'

'Of course, Baba Yaga,' said Vasilisa.

The next day the same thing happened. Vasilisa sat down and sobbed, and she shared what little she had with her doll. The doll again told Vasilisa to sleep and that she would complete the task for her.

Vasilisa trusted the doll once more, and the doll did complete the task. Again Vasilisa awoke to the thundering hooves and the grinding of the pestle and mortar. She found that the peas and the poppy seeds had been separated and that the doll was back in her pocket.

There was no disguising Baba Yaga's anger this time. She was furious and she didn't care if she had made a deal or not. She had again been cheated out of a meal. This time she told Vasilisa to go and chop enough wood to make a roaring fire beneath her cauldron.

Vasilisa now knew she would not make it home unless she tried to escape. She took out her doll, who had not failed her, and she asked her doll what she should do.

How could she get past the creaking hinges on the door? How on earth would she get past the long branches of the tree? How would she avoid the claws of the cat and how would she manage to calm the dog?

Of course, the little doll told her how, and Vasilisa collected a small pie from the pantry, a bone from beside the fire, took a ribbon from her doll's hair and a tiny can of oil that sat on the mantelpiece. When the fire was hot and Baba Yaga was fast asleep in front of it, thinking Vasilisa was in the wood store, Vasilisa made her escape.

She used the oil on the creaking hinges of the door, which had never been shown such attention before and opened easily for her. She tied the ribbon in the birch tree, which had never been given such gifts before and drew back from barring her way. Next the dog was calmed with the offering of the bone and the cat by the pie, purring as it ate.

She was out of the hut, but where was she to go next? The forest was so dark.

'Vasilisa, do not worry,' said the little doll, her voice once more reassuring Vasilisa. 'Take one of the skulls from the fence and I will show you the way home.'

And the little doll did. Vasilisa got all the way to her house, where her mother and sisters were still, days later, sitting in the dark. At last, she had the flame that had been asked of her, but she did not want to scare her sisters with the skull and the flame inside it, so she went to put it outside the house.

'No, no,' said the little doll from her pocket. 'Take it inside; that's what they wanted.'

As soon as the mother and the sisters laid eyes on that skull with the flame that had come from Baba Yaga's hut, it burnt them to a cinder. They were nothing but three piles of ash.

'Now go from this house, Vasilisa,' said the doll. 'Go to the next town and there you will find an old woman who will look after you.'

Vasilisa did, the old woman took her in and treated her with kindness and compassion, and soon Vasilisa was taught a trade. Vasilisa learnt how to spin flax and the elder woman taught her how to weave. Vasilisa started to weave the flax that she had spun into the finest shirts you have ever seen.

Soon word reached the Tsar of what she had created and that they were befitting royalty. The Tsar called for a shirt to be brought to him and the fine weaving and softness against his skin was luxurious. Never had he seen craftsmanship like this before. He called for the person who had created it to come and see him, thinking he would employ them in the palace as his personal tailor.

When Vasilisa appeared at the palace, the Tsar saw the love and the goodness that shone from her. He fell in love with her and of course they married. Eventually Vasilisa's father returned from his work in far-flung lands and he heard the story of how his daughter had become the Tsar's wife. He went to live with them in the palace, was grateful to Vasilisa's little doll and, safe to say, he never married again.

CANDLE MAGIC

In May's chapter I showed you a simple ritual for welcoming back the sun and recognising its power. Candles have always had a homely, welcoming feel about them and a candle in the window often guided travellers home.

These days it's easy to make your own candles with a plethora of candle-making kits available online and you may even find candle-making workshops near you. There are also many makers of handmade, eco-friendly, soy candles who get very creative with the scents available and the subsequent names for them. So instead of giving you a candle-making 'how to', for this activity I am sharing with you how you might use candles to summon the light and bring yourself good luck and prosperity in what can be the darkest days of winter.

Candles create a focus for what you intend to achieve, and intention can be a powerful kind of magic. Blowing out the candle on your birthday cake and making a wish is a magical idea. But remember to use positivity to achieve your goals, not negativity.

Before you start, consider the burning time of your candle and how you are going to use it. Does it matter if you blow it out, or does it need to burn itself out? If so, are you going to be in the room with it?

Tea lights have the shortest burn time and most candles you buy will tell you what the burn time is on them. Many large handmade candles can burn for up to forty hours, so do bear this in mind.

Colours and scents in combination can be seen to correspond to the four elements of nature. For instance, green and pine scents connect with the forest and ultimately the element of earth, which is good for grounding goals and staying practical. Yellow and marigold might represent fire; blue and salt, water; white and sweet spice, the air.

The colours of candles are said to have certain associations, which you could correspond with any goals you might have:

White – neutral, cleansing and harmonious
Red – strength and passion
Blue – health and emotions
Green – finances
Yellow/gold – happiness and prosperity
Purple – powerful, peaceful, psychological
Black – protection

Candle scents can correspond to goals in similar ways:

Cinnamon – prosperity
Sage and rosemary – memory
Lavender – healing
Bay and juniper – protection

You could even create a sigil or seal to carve into the side of your candle. A simple way to do this is to write down what you intend to achieve as a sentence. Then cross out any repeated letters until you are left with only the ones that are not repeated. Write these letters together so that they form a shape. Choose a candle with an appropriate colour and scent, transfer this shape to a candle, say aloud what your intention is, and light the candle.

DECEMBER

ECLIPSE

THIS MORNING AS I SIT in my spot, thin wisps of sunlight attempting to pierce the winter-born clouds, the sun and the moon are once more in the sky at the same time. It's a full moon, lit by the atmospheric light. The sun will rise above the tree line in front of me. This is the furthest south it will rise before coming back north. In the summer it will rise above the trees to my left.

We have just under eight hours of daylight in December and this month holds the shortest day, the winter solstice, which many celebrate on or around the 21st.

The sun appears quickly as it always does, surprising me with the speed with which it flings itself into the sky, although at this time of year it never rises much higher than the tree line. As usual, there is a cacophony of corvids just before its arrival: jackdaws, crows and rooks.

It is said that if a person who is unwell should overhear a crow calling, it will mean certain death. I am pleased to be in good health and fine fettle this morning for this chorus. Crows, in particular, have long been associated with death. Infamously, a group of crows is called a murder. The Morrigan, in Welsh mythology, is often found in the company of crows, and for this shapeshifting goddess of death, the crow is her favourite form to appear in.

If we take a more philosophical view of this song, though, perhaps crows are particularly noisy this morning as they are calling in the death of the year and the end of the dark days. Once January arrives, we will gain light at an average of two minutes a day as the earth continues its slow turn towards the sun and summer once more.

In amongst the caws is the chatter of jackdaws and the crack of rooks' voices. The Anglo-Saxons called rooks *hroc*, which means 'croaker'; an apt name. Rooks are more welcome than crows in our folklore, as to lose a rookery from your land means that bad fortune will follow.

The frosted dew on the grass glows orange with the rising sun, and the sun climbs higher, yellowing the horizon. A bright blue sky emerges from the dark, and lines of candyfloss-pink mare's tail clouds spread out across it. These wispy tails are associated with incoming weather fronts, and sailors would lower their sails when they encountered these clouds out at sea. But I am safe here on the hillside and there is no sign of the weather turning just yet.

The sun may be up but it's still biting cold, or as they say in Hampshire, I am shrammed 'frozen with cold'. I huddle into my duck-down coat, hold my warm coffee cup close and I am grateful once more for the ski trousers keeping in some of the warmth.

I wonder if Persephone is as cold during her six months below the earth in the company of Hades. Hers is the most literal of seasonal lives because, as the Greek myth I mentioned in the January chapter tells us, Hades will only ever let her return to the surface for six months at a time. For the other six, when she is below the ground, the earth is left in winter.

The ancient Chinese medical text, *The Yellow Emperor's Classic of Internal Medicine*, talks of the virtues of light and how we must pay attention to the seasons in order to get the best from ourselves and preserve our health. For the Emperor, winter was a time for rest, as in Greek myth it is for Persephone. I always find December such a busy time of year with the rituals and celebrations our modern lives hold. So, I try to take time out on the solstice and that is what I am doing here this morning. Taking in the sun on the shortest day of the year.

As mentioned in the June chapter, during the solstices the sun slows down in its path. It rises and sets in pretty much the same place for a few days, as opposed to the rest of the year when it rises in a slightly different place – that's why it's called a solstice, roughly translating from Latin as 'sun stands still'.

This was so apparent to our ancestors that, as we saw in the July chapter, they built ancient circles of megaliths to celebrate both the summer and the winter standstills.

There are monuments and megaliths across the world that have been built purely to mark the sunrise on the winter solstice. We know this because they were built in a place where, at this time of year, we can see that the sun rises above a specific landmark, a spire, a mountain or between two stones, placed there by people long ago.

New Grange in County Meath, Ireland, is a very famous example of this. It is a Stone Age tomb constructed more than 1,000 years before Stonehenge. Through a small window, known as a roof-box, above the entrance passage, sunlight enters the burial chamber and travels down the passage to illuminate the chamber, 19m further on.

In Egypt, the Karnak Temple at Luxor is another example of humans building a temple that aligns with the sunrise on the winter solstice. For the ancient Egyptians this was a sanctuary to the sun god Ra, and as the sun rises it moves round towards the temple of Hatshepsut, which celebrates a female pharaoh. This further evidences the close relationship between pharaohs and the sun god Ra that we have seen in previous chapters.

In Cambodia, Angkor Wat is a Hindu–Buddhist temple celebrating the god Vishnu, the supreme being. If you stand at the western entrance as the sun rises on the winter solstice, you will see that it rises above the middle tower of the temple.

The ancient Inca people's citadel of Machu Picchu, Peru, also celebrates the winter solstice. Here the sun rises in the cleft of two of the surrounding mountains, and shines on the temple of the sun.

Remnants of winter sun celebrations can be found in the Nazca deserts, in the geoglyphs left by the Paracas people living there thousands of years ago. These lines, shapes and symbols are thought to mark the path of the sun at the solstice.

Many of us still celebrate the winter solstice at one of these sacred sites, but there are other ways we celebrate that are much closer to home. Across Europe, we sing in the season of winter with Yuletide songs and carols, and in this way, we sing back the light into the world in the darkest days of winter.

The first recorded song celebrating the seasons is attributed secular origins. It was recorded in the thirteenth century and is called 'Sumer is icumen in', translated as 'Summer has come in'. It celebrates the life that summer has brought with it, the first cuckoo, the lambs in the field; it even, amusingly, mentions a farting goat – a rip-roaring singing-in of the season.

As we have seen throughout this book, the changes observed in the position of the sun were of great significance to the ancient peoples of the world. They observed the sun, moon and stars closely and there is a strong link between archeoastronomy and mythology. This was not just in the case of the solar festivals: vernal equinox, summer solstice, autumnal equinox and winter solstice. Rarer occurrences such as solar eclipses also held great importance, this time more as portents and omens than as celebrations.

It must have been terrifying the first time a solar eclipse was noted. These communities knew how important the sun was, they worshipped it for this reason, and so for it to disappear, for them to have felt the cold that replaced it, the lack of birdsong and the stillness in the air, must have been confusing and frightening. These days we know it will pass and certainly in the UK a total solar eclipse is a very rare phenomenon.

In August 1999 I was lucky enough to witness a total solar eclipse. I heard the day become silent and I felt that chill in my bones as the moon and the sun lined up perfectly, the moon blocking out the light almost completely. The next solar eclipse here in the UK is slated for September 2090; not in my lifetime but I hope in my daughter's.

They may be rare for us in the UK but elsewhere in the world total or partial solar eclipses are a regular occurrence, with one visible from some point on the earth approximately every eighteen months.

For the Mexica people, dawn itself was a time of trepidation; would the sun continue to move across the sky? I love this belief that every day is a gift. The gods had blessed them once more with the reappearance of the sun.

The mythology and folklore surrounding the disappearance of the sun due to a solar eclipse usually involves something or someone eating the sun. In Ireland, a three-day solar eclipse was said to be the result of the Tuatha Dé Dannan descending to the earth from the heavens. In Indonesia, it is an angry giant who has eaten the sun. In Vietnam, an eclipse is called a *Nhật Thực*, encompassing the verb 'to eat', which refers to the myth that the sun has been eaten by a giant toad. In China, too, the name for the solar eclipse encompasses the word 'eat' in the phrase *ri shi*. This time it is a dog who eats the sun. In both China and Indonesia, cymbals, drums and gongs are played to encourage the giant or the dog to relinquish the sun, and they are played until the sun reappears. Many traditions and rituals surrounding eclipses, across the world, also involve apotropaic magic – the protecting of the home from evil spirits.

The Norse creation story tells of how the three brother gods, Odin, Villi and Ve, who created Midguard, or earth as we know it, took Sol and her brother Mani and placed them in the sky, riding in chariots with the orbs of the sun and the moon behind them. Sol carries the flaming sun and Mani the ice-cold moon. Two wolves, Sköll and Hati, snap at their feet. The horses that pull Sol's chariot are Arvak, meaning 'early riser', and Allsvin, meaning 'swift'. The sun she holds in her chariot was made from the sparks of Muspelheim, the land of fire, and Sol rides with her shield between the sun and the earth to stop the earth burning up. The wolf Sköll occasionally catches up with Sol, causing a full or partial solar eclipse. Hati plays the same part in lunar eclipses.

Although the names Sol and Sunna are often used interchangeably, Sol is usually Sunna's mother. They are nature goddesses or Vanir. These deities are also associated with fate and can be either benevolent, antagonistic or even protective spirits. When Sköll finally catches Sol, she will give birth to Sunna. Sunna will inherit her mother's powers and take the light into the new world.

As I walk back across the fields and through the woods, I spot many black feathers on the ground. More evidence of the local corvids. A crow's feather on the ground at your feet is supposed to be good luck, but they also remind me of Odin's ravens, Huginn and Muninn. These ravens scour the corners of the nine worlds collecting gossip in order to keep the All Father, Odin, informed. Perhaps this is where the rooks go each day as they fly over the ridge of trees I sit opposite. On a morning when Sol and Mani are in the sky together and the call of corvids hangs in the morning air, it is of course the Norse creation myth that I wish to share with you.

NORSE CREATION STORY

In the beginning there was darkness. Cold, black, sooty darkness; not sooty like ash, you understand, for this was a beginning not an end. Dark like the womb that will soon hold life, unknown like the sun to a pup who cannot yet see, empty like a forest not yet grown. Cold, black, sooty darkness.

Into this darkness, from Muspell in the south, came fire-bringing warmth to kindle new life, and from the north in Niflheim came ice to temper its destruction. Where they met, they disappeared, losing their former selves, down into Ginnungagap; the yawning gap, the maw of creation, a mighty chasm.

Further north, from the swirling mists and clawing cold of Niflheim, sprang a well and from that well flowed Élivágar, the eleven rivers of Hvergelmir: Svöl, Gunnþró, Fjörm, Fimbulþul, Sliðr, Hrið, Sylgr, Ylgr, Við, the holy Leiptr and Gjöll.

Relentlessly they travelled towards the gap, across the ice and fire, taking with them cinder, slag and slush to fill Ginnungagap. They created a river within that gap, where the ice and fire mixed with the waters and met to fill the nooks and crannies of that giant crevasse. Here it was said to be as 'mild as the windless sky'.

There were three wells in the worlds. We have seen in the north that Niflheim held one, the gap itself became another and the third lay in the south, in a plain called Helheim. This well was the source of warmth for the worlds to be.

As the well of Ginnungagap rose up, it brought with it a golden seed. The seed travelled with the waters up to the top of the worlds and grew into a tree. This tree was the Yggdrasil, the tree from which all plants would have their origins.

Three of this mighty plant's roots were set, one each into the three wells, and within its mighty arboreous arms sat an eagle who held the knowledge of all things. At the base of the tree, the dragon Nidhog nibbled at the roots and between the two ran Ratatoskr, a gossiping squirrel who conveyed messages from one to another. Four mighty stags, Dáinn, Dvalinn, Duneyrr and Duraþrór, nibbled at the leaves, and the morning dew that rested on their horns further replenished the rivers of the worlds.

In Ginnungagap, life was forming once more. From the ice came the first of the Jotun, Ymir, a gigantic man, fetid and sweating, alone in his being. From the sweat that formed on his skin as he slept, his children Mimir and Bestla were born, and they in turn birthed generations of Jotuns, a nation of giants.

From the swirling mists, a mighty auroch appeared, an enormous cow named Audumla, and from her came four rivers of milk to sustain the Jotuns and their children. It was an onerous task and Audumla licked the ice to quench her thirst.

As she did so, another form appeared from the ice. She licked the ice and on the first day, there was a mass of golden hair; on the second, a man's head emerged; and on the third day, the man pulled himself from the ice and drank the milk of Audumla. This was Buri and his son would be Bor. Bor married Bestla and they in turn had three children, half-god and half-giant: Odin, Vili and Ve.

From the first day they laid eyes on the Jotuns, the brothers were set against them, and once they had grown and after many battles, the three brothers were the death of Ymir, that first, fetid, steaming giant. Ymir's blood ran thick and fast, and his kind were drowned in it, unable to hold back its tide. Those who survived were banished to the land known as Jotunheim.

Looking around them at the destruction they had caused, the brothers had to find a way to put right this horror. They needed to make something new out of the debris.

From Ymir's skull they created the sky, by placing the corners on the four corners of the earth. Ymir's brains became the clouds and who knows what thoughts they hold now? Finally, the glowing embers of Muspell were used to create the sun, the moon and the stars. This was Midgard, the land of humankind.

From the roots of the great ash Yggdrasil came Ask and Embla, the first man and woman. Villi put blood in their veins; Ve, thoughts in their heads; and Odin, the All Father, breathed life into their lungs.

Next the brothers turned to Jotunheim once more, and from the giants that were left, they took a mother and son, Night and Day. They were each placed in a chariot destined to ride around the world as it turns.

The brothers had one last task to allocate and so from Midgard they took two humans, Sol and Mani. Mani would carry the moon and Sol would carry the sun, both in horse-drawn carriages. They travel across our skies, each chased by a solitary wolf, Sköll and Hati. They snap at their heels, and when they finally catch them and swallow the orbs, that will be the day to end all days: Ragnarök.

SOLSTICE CAKE

Fruited Christmas cakes of the UK, chocolate Yule logs of France, Italian sweet panettone or La Befana cake that honours the old witch of winter, the German Stollen that hides chunks of bright marzipan, Chile's fruited pan de Pascua, Spain's almond-stuffed turron, Portuguese king cake, the wreath-shaped kransekake and pin-wheel Joulutorttu of Scandinavia, the sweet potato and pumpkin pies of the USA, the sweet rice and coconut bibingka cakes eaten in the Philippines … wherever you are, across the world, this time of year is cake-baking time.

I'm partial to a Battenberg cake, possibly because the two-tone colours remind me of the days I spent with my mum, making marble cakes. Battenberg has the added bonus of marzipan, though, and it's no secret that I love marzipan.

The Battenberg cake is sometimes called church-window cake or domino cake because of its checkerboard construction. Marzipan is thought to have originated from Arabia, although there are varying stories attributing its invention to different countries in Europe.

Marzipan's main ingredients are almonds and sugar. The almond tree is one of the first trees to flower in the spring and therefore it is often associated with the rituals and customs of fertility and rebirth that occur at this time of year. So, what better cake to remind us of the spring that is to come than one covered in marzipan?

I've created this version of a Battenberg to celebrate the light and the dark with a chocolate orange batter and a lemon batter. Once you have covered the cake in the marzipan, you could add the rune for the sun, Sowilo, on the top. You can see how I've done this in the example on the website page that accompanies this book, detailed in the introduction.

I have made this cake using a Battenberg tin, but you could make it by first making two small, rectangular cakes, cutting them in half lengthways and then layering them in the traditional Battenberg pattern, or by layering the batter in a loaf tin.

Ingredients

125g of butter
125g of caster sugar
2 medium eggs, beaten
50g of ground almonds
100g of self-raising flour
A pinch of salt
30g of cocoa powder
Zest and juice of one large orange
Zest and juice of one lemon
100g of apricot jam
A small amount of icing sugar for dusting
500g of marzipan
A small amount of caster sugar for sprinkling

Method

- Set your oven to 180°C/160°C fan oven or Gas 4.
- Line the Battenberg tin with baking parchment.
- Soften the butter in a large bowl.
- Then add the sugar, flour, almonds, salt and eggs into a large bowl and, using a handheld electric mixer, combine until light and fluffy.
- Place half of the mixture into another bowl. Try to be as accurate as you can, weighing if possible.

- Add the lemon zest and lemon juice to one bowl and the orange zest, juice and cocoa powder to the other.
- Share the lemon-flavoured mixture between two of the Battenberg sections and do the same with the chocolate orange mixture.
- Bake in the middle of the oven for up to 25 minutes until the tops of the cakes spring back to the touch, taking care as they will be hot.
- Once the sponges are completely cool, check they are all of equal length, trimming if necessary.
- Warm the apricot jam in a pan on a low heat.
- Using some of the warmed jam, construct the checkerboard pattern of the Battenberg.
- Put the cake to one side and on a clean surface, dusted with icing sugar, knead the marzipan and then roll it out so that it is wide enough to cover your Battenberg cake.
- Spread the rest of the apricot jam across the marzipan and then roll the cake up carefully in the marzipan, trimming off any excess.
- Sprinkle with a touch of caster sugar and serve your solstice cake with a cup of your favourite tea.

ACKNOWLEDGEMENTS

Thank you for joining me on my sunrise vigils. I hope you have enjoyed this journey through the year with the sun as our guide and that it has inspired you to greet the sun as it rises at least once in the year; the one past or the year to come.

Many people have helped to make this book possible: my good friend Tiffany Francis-Baker who wrote the wonderful foreword; Elinor Newman who checked the science; Dave Tipper who accompanied me for November's sunrise and helped me to see the sun in a different light; my family who supported me when I holed myself away in the study for hours on end, writing and editing, or crept out of the front door at 4.30 a.m. in search of the sun; the team at The History Press who breathed life into the manuscript and produced the book you now hold in your hands. Thank you all.

I am for ever grateful to the earth and the sun for the wonders they have shown me during the course of this project, for warming my bones on those bitterly cold mornings and for holding a space for me. Finally, I thank all those people before me, who held the stories of the sun and passed them down through the generations, so that I have been able to share them with you in these pages.

ABOUT THE AUTHOR

 Dawn Nelson lives within the beautiful South Downs. Her specialism is landscape, heritage and nature interpretation. She works with heritage sites, museums, schools, outdoor educators, community groups, councils and libraries to bring the world around us to life through story.

She has worked with the South Downs National Park Authority, Butser Ancient Farm, Gilbert White's House & Gardens, Weald & Downland Museum as well as many other organisations in Hampshire and Sussex. You can find her performing stories at events such as boat burnings, Beltane celebrations and multi-period re-enactment shows. Her passion is connecting people with nature, history and the landscape that surrounds them, through storytelling, and you can keep up to date with Dawn's work by visiting her website www.ddstoryteller.co.uk, where you will find her newsletter, podcast, news and upcoming events.

BIBLIOGRAPHY

Ashe, Russell, et al. (1973) *Folklore: Myths and Legends of Britain*, Reader's Digest, London.

Baker, Margaret (2018) *Discovering the Folklore of Plants*, Shire Publications, Oxford.

Barber, Richard (1992) *Bestiary: MS Bodley 764*, The Folio Society, London.

Berresford, Ellis (2002) *The Mammoth Book of Celtic Myths and Legends*, Robinson, London.

Borges, Jorge Luis (2002) *The Book of Imaginary Beings*, Vintage, London.

Chopra, Deepak (2020) *Total Meditation*, Penguin Random House, London.

Colarusso, John (2002) *Nart Sagas: Ancient Myths and Legends of the Circassians and Abkhazians*, Princeton University Press, Oxford.

Culpeper, Nicholas (2007) *Culpeper's Complete Herbal and English Physician* (first published 1653), Applewood Books, Carlisle, MA.

Dell, Christopher (2012) *Mythology: An Illustrated Journey into Our Imagined Worlds*, Thames & Hudson, New York.

Dent, Susie (2018) *Brewer's Dictionary of Phrase and Fable*, 20th edition, Hachette, London.

Douglas, Faith (2020) *The Nature Remedy*, HarperCollins, London.

Egerkrans, Johan (2013) *Vaesen: Spirits and Monsters of Scandinavian Folklore*, Balto Print, Vilnius, Lithuania.

Forest, Danu (2016) *The Magical Year*, Watkins, London.

Fort, Tom (2019) *The A303: Highway to the Sun*, Simon & Schuster, London.

Geddes, Linda (2019) *Chasing the Sun: The New Science of Sunlight and How It Shapes Our Bodies and Minds*, Wellcome Collection, Profile Books, Croydon.

Geoffrey of Monmouth (1966) *The History of the Kings of Britain*, Penguin, Basingstoke.

Glassie, Henry (1985) *Irish Folktales*, Pantheon Books, New York.

Guest, Charlotte (1838–45) *The Mabinogion*.

Harrington-Oakley, Christina (2020) *The Treadwell's Book of Plant Magic*, Treadwell's Books, London.

Jones, Steve (2019) *Here Comes the Sun*, Little Brown, London.

Larrington, Caroline (2015) *The Land of the Green Man*, Bloomsbury, London.

Monaghan, Patricia (2014) *Encyclopedia of Goddesses and Heroines*, New World Library, Novato, CA.

Murphy, Anthony and Moore, Richard (2020) *Island of the Setting Sun*, The Liffey Press, Dublin.

Norroena Society, The (2009) *The Ásatrú Edda: Sacred Lore of the North*, Bloomington, IN.

Nozedar, Adele (2010) *The Illustrated Signs and Symbols Sourcebook: An A to Z Compendium of Over 1000 Designs*, Harper Thorsons, London.

Owens, Brendan (2021) *The Sun*, Royal Observatory Greenwich, London.

Patterson, Rachel (2016) *Pagan Portals: The Cailleach*, Moon Books, New Alresford, Hampshire.

Philips, Charles (2005) *The Lost History of Aztec and Maya*, Anness Publishing, London.

Pitt, Frances (1944) *Wild Animals in Britain*, B. T. Batsford, London.

Quirke, Stephen (2001) *The Cult of Ra: Sun-Worship in Ancient Egypt*, Thames & Hudson, London.

Struthers, Jane (2009) *Red Sky at Night: The Book of Lost Countryside Wisdom*, Ebury Press, London.

Swainson, Charles (2004) *The Folklore and Provincial Names of British Birds* (first published 1885), Kessinger Publishing, Whitefish, MT.

Telyndru, Jhenah (2020) *Pagan Portals: Blodeuwedd*, Moon Books, New Alresford, Hampshire.

Thomas, Taffy (2019) *The Magpie's Nest: A Treasury of Bird Folk Tales*, The History Press, Cheltenham.

Thoreau, Henry David (2017) *Walden* (first published 1854), Vintage, London.

Tongue, Ruth L. (1970) *Forgotten Folk-Tales of the English Counties*, Routledge Library Editions, London.

Wallis, Faith (1999) *Bede: The Reckoning of Time*, Liverpool University Press, Liverpool.

White, Gilbert (1789) *The Natural History of Selbourne*, available at https://www.gutenberg.org/files/1408/1408-h/1408-h.htm.

Wilde, Lady Jane (1887) *Ancient Legends, Mystic Charms and Superstitions of Ireland*, available at https://www.gutenberg.org/ebooks/61436.

Woolf, Jo (2022) *Britain's Birds: A Treasury of Fact, Fiction and Folklore*, National Trust, Swindon.

Woolf, Jo (2020) *Britain's Trees: A Treasury of Traditions, Superstitions, Remedies and Literature*, National Trust, Swindon.

WEBSITES

BBC Wildlife: https://www.discoverwildlife.com

British Library: https://www.bl.uk

British Museum: Bronze Age Myth of the Sun Cycle from Scandinavia | Curator's Corner S7 Ep4, https://www.youtube.com/watch?v=ftMtrgHoqEU

British Museum: The World of Stonehenge Exhibition, 17 February–17 July 2022, https://www.britishmuseum.org/

British Trust for Ornithology: https://www.bto.org/

Crankie Factory: http://www.thecrankiefactory.com

Hypertext (for translations of the 'Song of Amergin'): http://www.thehypertexts.com/Song%20of%20Amergin%20Modern%20English%20Translation.htm

NASA (for all things space and solar system related): https://www.nasa.gov

Project Britain (for UK festivals): http://projectbritain.com

Royal Museums Greenwich – https://www.rmg.co.uk – For all things time related

RSPB – https://www.rspb.org.uk - For UK bird knowledge

South Downs National Park – https://www.southdowns.gov.uk

Te Kete Ipurangi (for 'How Māui Slowed the Sun'): https://eng.matauranga-maori.tki.org.nz/Support-materials/Te-Reo-Maori/Maori-Myths-Legends-and-Contemporary-Stories/How-Maui-slowed-the-sun

Time & Date (for getting up at the right time for sunrises): https://www.timeand-date.com

Wildlife Trusts: https://www.wildlifetrusts.org

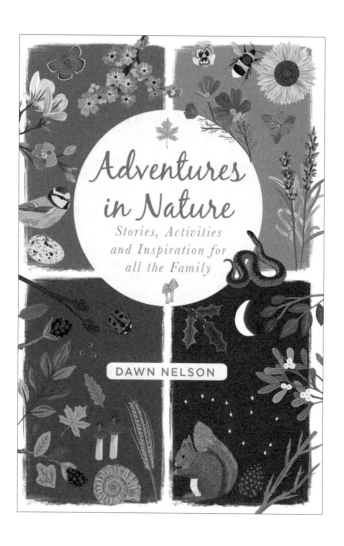

Adventures
in Nature
*Stories, Activities
and Inspiration for
all the Family*

DAWN NELSON